Murder out of the Blue

Steve Turnbull

Murder out of the Blue
By Steve Turnbull

ISBN 978-0-9534886-2-9

Published by Tau Press Ltd.

Cover art by Drew Northcott

To my family (you know who you are).

Acknowledgements

My beta-readers for their forebearance, and my wife for being an honest alpha-reader and knowing more about India than I do.

CHAPTER 1

Maliha Anderson glanced down at her watch. They were late. The *RMS Macedonia* was scheduled to launch at three o'clock local time, half-an-hour away, and the great Peninsular & Oriental Steam Navigation Company were strict about their schedules. She looked out at the sun-bleached streets of Khartoum, almost devoid of life in the heat of the day. Flat roofs all of a height except the domes and minarets of the mosques. To the west the sun's light shimmered on the rippling surface of the White Nile.

She leaned forward against the polished wooden rail that curved around the stern viewing lounge of 'B' Deck. 'A' Deck above—for the truly wealthy—had a similar lounge but fewer and larger berths. Those in the cheaper second and third class berths below had no lounge at all; only the Promenade and Observation decks were available to them with no privacy to speak of.

All together they were 300 souls packed into a steel and glass container thundering through the sky at 100 miles per hour and an altitude of 3000ft courtesy of the Faraday device and the steam-driven rotors on the ends of the six stubby wings.

The Purser had given them a tour after they had lifted from London three days ago. The *Macedonia* was the latest passenger vessel of the P&O line, and flaunted in its newspaper advertisements as a marvel of the skies: a floating Sky Liner with its rotors to take it vertically into the clouds then swivel to drive the vessel across the firmament. It was, they said, a miracle of engineering.

Maliha sighed. Always they were "miracles of engineering". Then she smiled. This truly was a miracle of engineering and it did indeed please her. She ran her fingers along the painted iron underside of the rail, feeling the bumps of the letters that spelt out the name of the Belfast shipbuilders: Harland and Wolfe.

Movement outside caught her eye.

The two lost sheep emerged in sudden colour against the washed out shades of ochre. They hurried arm in arm towards the ramp. The Welsh copper heiress Temperance Williams, intense with the certainty of a *zenana* missionary, travelling to India to save the souls of the Hindu womenfolk. And beside her was Lochana Modi primarily nurse and attendant to General Makepeace-Flynn. It seemed Temperance had decided to begin her missionary work with Lochana.

They were unaccompanied again. It had been the same in Constantinople. Temperance was a very modern young woman and did not consider a male escort to be required under any circumstance. And it seemed the General did not mind his nurse going ashore with her; certainly he felt no compunction in co-opting Maliha to push his wheelchair, despite her injury. He seemed to think that because she was young, just nineteen, he could ignore her need for a walking stick when in port.

"The wanderers have returned, eh?"

Maliha did not turn to look at the General who rolled into place beside her, propelled by a steward. He pulled on the cigar clenched in his claw-like fingers and blew a cloud of white smoke at the glass. He ordered the steward to fetch him a whiskey, and the man slid away like a ghost. Maliha leaned forward to watch as the women approached the ship.

The two figures outside reached the shadow of the liner. One of the ship's officers appeared from the belly of the vessel and strode down the ramp. He offered his arm to Miss Williams. She ignored him and marched into the ship without even a sideways glance.

"Certainly has her own mind that filly," the General said. Maliha did not need to see the grin on his face to know it was there. "Needs taking in hand. Touch of the crop, eh?"

"Excuse me, General." Maliha took up her walking stick from where it leant against the ironwork. Before he had the opportunity to say something even less decent, or call her back, she turned away and limped briskly towards her cabin.

She slipped between the wing-backed red leather chairs that would not have looked out of place in a gentlemen's club, their backs so high one could disappear into them. She strode past the bar on the port-side and, beyond that, the small but eclectic library. Not that there was a great deal of time to read on this trip as she was only travelling as far as Ceylon. They would arrive in a couple of days, but those heading on to Australia had another week to occupy themselves, plenty of time to become bored with deck quoits.

But, she admitted to herself as she stepped into the stairwell that climbed up to the Observation deck she had yet to grow tired of the ship launching itself into the blue. It was not as elegant as a seagull catching the uprising winds against a cliff and hovering in space, but it was a "miracle of engineering". And, once in flight, the strain on her leg was so reduced she could forego her stick completely. As there was no one nearby, she allowed herself a smile.

ii

The ship's warning klaxon sounded with two long bursts indicating the Faraday device would be engaged in just two minutes. Maliha was one of very few people on the Promenade deck; those that were there scattered along both port and starboard sides, peering through the gleaming glass that protected them from the outside air. Most passengers disliked the transition to light-weight when the device was activated; they would be in their bunks, in their beds, or at least in chairs. Maliha enjoyed the tranquillity and the unspoken camaraderie among those souls who braved the event.

She took her place leaning against the rail that separated her from the wide expanse of glass and steel stretching overhead and fully enclosing the open decks. The emptiness of Khartoum had been replaced by crowds, five or six deep, around the perimeter of the air-port, like a multi-coloured ribbon surrounding them.

Beneath her, through the glass, distributed along the ship's hull, were the three port-side wings; each one perhaps half the width of the ship again. At the end of each wing, enclosed in sheaths of beaten steel, were the massive steam-turbines that drove the rotors. For landing and take-off the turbines were turned to the vertical position with the rotors parallel to the ground.

The klaxon sounded a single long blast: one minute to go. The ship shook as steam tore through the pipes and into the turbines. The rotors resisted for a moment then reluctantly began to rotate. At first she could follow the individual movements of the blades but they accelerated quickly and were soon nothing but a semi-transparent blur glittering in the sunlight.

The klaxon gave three short blasts. There was a count of ten and the Faraday device was engaged. The sensation was like being at the top of a swing, about to descend. It was like falling without movement. It was not uncommon for people to feel sick at least initially but Maliha revelled in it; it felt like freedom. It was only three days before, when she had felt this for the first time travelling in the atmospheric train from Bournemouth to London, then in the underground Tube and finally this ship itself. Now she was an old hand.

Further along the deck, near the enclosed Ladies Reading Room, a young lad—perhaps only ten years old—leapt into the air and touched the ceiling of the Observation deck. His father, his clothing marking him as third class, caught him as he descended with the lightness of a bird.

The rotation of the propellers increased. The ferocious down-gusting wind from them whipped up clouds of dust and sand, but the glass dome that enclosed the whole of the upper decks protected them; while outside, Khartoum became nothing but a phantom beyond the ship's own private sandstorm.

The ship listed to port slightly, and she felt herself pushed against the rail. This was it. Somewhere adjustments were made; valves opened or closed by tiny amounts to adjust the ship's attitude, and the deck straightened once more. The rotor noise increased again. She knew they were airborne now, but the wind-driven sand filled the air around the ship.

Then they rose above it. Khartoum lay below with its streets laid out in the form of the Union Jack—the legacy of Lord Kitchener. The Blue and White Nile rivers reflected the intense sunlight. The clouds of sand drifted along the streets but settled out quickly. The ribbon of people had become a ribbon of upturned faces. She resisted the urge to wave back to the children that ran back and forth below them, though in her heart she was as excited as they.

The klaxon sounded once more to indicate a successful launch followed by the ship's steam siren that blasted their farewell to Africa. The ground below twisted as the ship changed its heading towards the East and slightly south to cross to the Red Sea, then it would turn south to follow the coast.

The central rotors swivelled a few degrees toward the horizontal, giving them forward propulsion and Khartoum slid away beneath them. Maliha lifted her walking stick, held it at its centre as she took bold steps, towards the bow and the Ladies Reading room. As she passed the enthusiastically bouncing boy, he paused and stared. Maliha heard the sotto voce words of a child that has not learned to whisper. "That lady's been out in the sun too long."

"Quiet."

"But why…"

She slipped into the reading room, mercifully empty. Most of the ladies would be suffering the vapours after the trauma of launch. This final refuge was near the prow of the ship, just behind the superstructure occupied solely by the Captain and his senior crew.

Although it was called a reading room, reading was perhaps the least indulged exercise. When it was occupied the most common activity was gossip, not that she was invited to take part—not that it would have been an undertaking she would have enjoyed. Being the subject of such malice quickly disabuses one of its merits.

"Excuse me, miss?"

Maliha jumped. There was a maid holding cutlery and a cleaning cloth.

"Yes?"

"This area is for first class passengers."

No escape. If only she had taken after her Father more than her Mother.

"I certainly hope so. Now if you will go about your own business. I will go about mine."

The girl's face reddened though whether from embarrassment or anger Maliha could not tell. She turned away and strode to the windows nearer the bow. It did not really matter anyway. In two days they'd be in Ceylon, and in another couple of days she would be back home. No more "respectable" women judging her by the colour of her skin.

The ship had reached its cruising altitude. The propellers were fully rotated to the horizontal and the ship threw itself through the clear blue sky. The sun hung almost directly above and ahead of them, in the distance, mountains peeked above the horizon.

The afternoon passed quietly. By three o'clock, the reading room boasted some twenty occupants from ladies as young as Maliha with their chaperones, to women of a certain age and beyond. She felt uncomfortable, there were too many pairs of eyes glancing in her direction.

Maliha took one last look at the African landscape gliding away beneath them to the thrumming of the six powerful turbines. The temperature inside the ship had dropped as the air they now breathed was vented from the outside and driven through by the pressure of their movement.

Light as a feather she managed a gentle bound across the room, successfully negotiating maiden aunts and highly strung debutantes. She smiled to herself as she took hold of the door handle, then composed her face to perfect neutrality as she opened it and stepped through on to a deck thronging with passengers from all classes.

She walked the length of the Promenade deck, skirting the central games area. High above, the triple domes of glass and riveted steel allowed the sun to pour through. A few hardy souls played quoits in the blazing light but nothing more energetic. Through the glass ceiling, she could see the starboard funnel, near the stern, churning out smoke from the furnaces. The speed of their progress ripping it into a horizontal trail.

iii

Maliha reached 'B' Deck through the port-side stern stairwell. She considered returning to the lounge as there was a good chance it would be empty at this time of day, or at least there would be a chair in which she could hide. She turned towards the stern but had gone only a few paces, long bouncing ones though they were, when she grabbed the brass rail to bring herself to a halt.

The afternoon sun and the porcelain sky were so bright that everything inside the lounge was nothing but shadow. Dark against the blinding backdrop was the wheelchair-bound figure of the General facing the slim silhouette of his nurse. As Maliha watched, the General gestured violently at her, his hand outstretched and open upwards. Lochana turned towards the window and took a step away.

The roared words of the General *don't you turn your back on me* penetrated the thrumming of the rotors. The rest of his words lost. Lochana turned back and took the General's hand, clasping it in both of hers. Maliha could almost imagine the touch as if it were some performance of Shakespeare, as if they were star-crossed lovers.

The outrageous ill-manners of her eavesdropping struck her. She turned on her heel embarrassed by her own behaviour and the scene she had witnessed. In an instant she resolved to return to her cabin, the real world was too full of emotion, too full of care to be easily borne. She tore herself away from the thing she should not have witnessed.

"Miss Anderson?" The sharp nasal tones of Mrs Barbara Makepeace-Flynn—a woman of few words and considerably less empathy—sliced the air. Maliha almost stumbled over her own feet as the woman emerged from the passageway that led to her cabin.

The General and his wife occupied separate cabins a short distance down the passage from Maliha's room. The nurse's cabin was next to the General's with an adjoining door. It was an arrangement that now took on a different meaning in Maliha's thoughts. The unbidden images that surfaced in her mind would have made a paler woman flush.

Not quite understanding her own motivations, Maliha took a few more steps before turning to speak to Mrs Makepeace-Flynn, arranging herself so the woman would have her back to the lounge, her husband and his nurse.

"Can I help you, Mrs Makepeace-Flynn?"

"You will accompany me to afternoon tea."

A lady did not eat in public without company. Maliha was in no doubt that if it had been Temperance Williams who had crossed Mrs Makepeace-Flynn's path she would have been a more acceptable choice. Miss Williams was a far better option with her Britishness unmistakably marked by her pale skin. As that wise child had commented, the best that could be said of Maliha was that she had been out in the sun too long: an offense almost as bad as having an Indian mother. The fact that her Brahmin mother was a member of the Indian aristocracy meant nothing to the pure blood British.

"You are too kind."

The woman harrumphed as if she were well aware of just how demeaning it would be for her. But Maliha was not paying attention. The lovers had moved further toward the wide expanse of glass at the rear of the vessel and out of sight behind a pillar with the General wheeling himself easily in the reduced gravity. But it was not they who caught her eye now, but the Indian-born steward who leaned out from behind the bar and stared unashamedly at the General and his nurse.

Another harrumph interrupted her and was also noticed by the steward who disappeared back into the bar. Maliha turned to see Mrs Makepeace-Flynn paused and waiting. Maliha fell into step half a pace behind the General's wife who did not deign to continue their conversation. Maliha knew she was a convenient sop to convention and nothing more.

iv

Maliha made her excuses to Mrs Makepeace-Flynn as soon as it was decent to do so: after two cups of tea and a delicious macaroon. She headed back to her cabin, calculating the hours to Ceylon in her head. It did not require any amount of cleverness to see why the General might prefer a younger woman over his wife. But that said, if one were treated so abominably by one's husband how could one not become bitter? The Bard had it right about tangled webs woven by deceit. One could only hope the outcome would not resemble those of the Bard's most famous tragedy.

Maliha unlocked and entered her cabin. While not one of the best first class accommodations it was far from unpleasant: a comfortable lounge area with sofa, armchairs and coffee table, a writing desk, a small book shelf, double bed behind a screen, large windows that could be opened in a pinch, and a separate room for one's toilet. A palace compared to the shared rooms of the boarding school.

She smiled as she placed her walking stick by the door. How pleasant it would have been if her room-mates had succeeded in their plans to have her removed to a room of her own. She arranged her skirts and sat lightly in an armchair, the large rectangular window giving her a clear view of the blue sky and brown earth of the Sudan. The prejudice of the other girls blinded them to the irony of their plan. The teachers, however, were not so blind and unfortunately the plan had not succeeded.

Still, best not to dwell on such things. Absently she rubbed her thigh through the layers of her dress. The ridges of the scar pressed into her skin though she could not feel them with her fingers. No, it is best not to dwell on the evil that could inhabit the minds of immature girls. A good Buddhist did not concern herself with material things. Nor did a good daughter of the Empire dwell on misfortune. Perhaps she should just remain in her room for the rest of the journey. She opened her copy of Romeo and Juliet, slipped the bookmark to one side and continued to read from where she had left off.

There came an abrupt rap on the door, interrupting Romeo's vengeance on Tybalt. Was it possible the universe connived against her? With a sigh, she lifted her feet from the comfort of the footstool and headed for the door. She glanced at herself in the usefully placed mirror by the door—her hair needed some attention but she would do.

"Who is it?"

"Temperance." Came the light Welsh-accented voice.

Maliha fixed on a smile and pulled open the door to the pretty and slightly flushed face of Temperance Williams. She had her ivory cigarette holder between her lips, inhaled deeply and removed it, holding it delicately in the fingers of her right hand. There was an awkward pause as if Temperance were waiting for something. She breathed out smoke.

"Do you want to come in?"

"No, no, *cariad*, I won't disturb you more than I must."

There followed another awkward silence; Temperance took another lungful of smoke and glanced up the companionway to where one of the maids had appeared around the corner, wiping handrails. Temperance looked down at the book still clasped in Maliha's hand.

"Do you have one of those Shakespeare plays I could borrow?"

Maliha suppressed her surprise. "Of course, any one in particular?"

Temperance glanced again at the maid. "Oh, I'm not so bothered. I just fancied something to read until dinner. Just like you. Thought I'd sit in the lounge. Something light?"

"Twelfth Night, perhaps?"

"Just the thing."

Maliha stepped away, feeling awkward leaving her visitor at the door. It took only a moment to find the volume. Temperance waited and watched. She reached out her hand as Maliha returned.

"A couple of hours of Shakespeare, what could be better?" With that, she turned away and bounced lightly past the maid and into the port-side companionway.

Maliha closed her door with a click, looking at the Do Not Disturb sign that hung on the inside handle wondering if she dared hang it outside the room in the middle of the day. "Indeed, a few quiet hours with Shakespeare. What could be better?"

CHAPTER 2

Maliha had no one to help her change for dinner. Most of the first class passengers came with at least one personal servant, if not an entire retinue. But she was not alone in doing without, even the General's wife had no one. Irascible she might be but she was self-sufficient. Or perhaps they simply could not afford it. They would rather travel first class without staff than second class. And the vessel did provide personnel on request. That, however, was a facility Maliha did not feel comfortable with. The school required them to look after themselves (although obviously the other girls had helped one another). This was no hardship.

She stared into the mirror one more time and adjusted her hair. She wondered whom she was trying to impress. Certainly no one on board this ship. But was it wrong to have pride in one's appearance? At what point did making oneself look pleasing turn into hubris? But was life itself not a form of art? Should one not deport oneself as pleasingly as possible?

She cut herself short by pulling open the door. She closed and locked it behind her, slipping the key into her reticule. It was twenty minutes before seven, enough time to order a drink in the lounge as the other passengers would do.

As she approached the junction between her side passage and the port-side companionway, she found her way barred by the steward she had noted earlier displaying the unexpected curiosity in the General's private conversation. He moved to block her way forcing her to arrest her motion by gripping the rail, but her momentum carried them inappropriately close. So close she could smell his breath. His wrinkled uniform seemed a size too large for him.

"Sahiba?" His voice was pitched high, and his eyes flicked nervously from somewhere near her feet to her face.

He did not seem menacing and Maliha suppressed her fears. The idea that anyone would attempt something unpleasant in such an open place was not sensible. But still she stepped back until a more suitable gap opened between them.

"What do you want?"

He put his hand in his pocket, pulled out a folded envelope and thrust it at her.

"For Lochan."

"Lochana Modi?"

The steward hesitated then nodded. "Hām." He spoke in Hindi.

With an effort, it had been a good many years, Maliha made her best effort to reply in kind, though her native tongue was Tamil. "Give it to her yourself."

Unfortunately that was the exact moment Mrs Makepeace-Flynn chose to float past. The older woman stared at the two of them—an eyebrow raised in admonishment—before her momentum carried her out of sight towards the lounge. Maliha was grateful the General's wife seemed unable to grasp the simple science behind movement in reduced gravity. She turned her attention back to the steward.

"I cannot." He pushed the letter into her hand, and she clutched it reflexively as it slipped away when he released it. He spun around and headed away from the lounge. He was clearly experienced at movement under the Faraday effect.

Maliha spread the envelope out in her hands. The name "Lochan Modi" was written in careful English in the centre. She turned it over and examined the back: it was one of the former mass-produced envelopes where the sticking was left to the purchaser. That was another deprivation living in India would impose, unless she chose to spend a great deal of money on the imported pre-gummed envelopes. In this case, the sender had chosen to seal the envelope with a large splash of common wax.

She wondered whether the sender was the steward or someone else. If it were the steward why had he not attempted to deliver it in the previous few days? The answer was clear enough even as the question presented itself. She did not recall seeing him before, therefore he had come aboard at Khartoum. His confidence on the vessel, however, indicated he was a genuine employee of the P&O line.

She examined the envelope again. The handwriting was quite precise, but the pen must be old as the letters were uneven and scratchy. Most likely written by one of the street-corner scribes she had seen in Puducherry when visiting with her mother.

ii

"Seen my nurse? Blasted chit's disappeared off somewhere."

The General hove into view, wheeling himself; no great exertion with the ship in flight although he still seemed to expect someone to do it for him if such a person were available. Maliha pushed the letter into her reticule, and when she looked up the practiced smile was once more on her face.

"I'm sorry, General, I have not seen her. I've been in my room since tea."

"Be a dear and shove me up to the lounge, would you? We'll see if she's there. Couldn't dress myself for dinner, had to get one of the ship's boys to give me a hand."

"Of course, General."

She got behind him and propelled him effortlessly to the lounge.

The buzz of polite conversation grew as they approached, small knots of people discussing everything and nothing. She scanned the room for the group to which they belonged. She spotted Mrs Makepeace-Flynn talking to the Spencers: Valerie and Maxwell. They were newlyweds moving out to the Fortress in Ceylon. He was an engineer engaged by one of the many companies that had sprung up around the British void-port, for the construction work of the Queen Victoria station hanging thousands of miles above Ceylon on the very edge of the void itself.

As they passed the bar Maliha glanced across to see if the steward was there. He wasn't.

"It's really terribly exciting." Maxwell Spencer's voice was the kind that penetrated background noise like an angry wasp or, in his case, a happy wasp. Maliha couldn't decide whether the perpetual bonhomie of the Spencers was genuine. "They keep the station with its Faraday device continually activated, and it stays up there at about 7,000 miles. We'll be able to see it on clear nights, I'm sure."

Maliha let the wheelchair roll to a gentle halt beside the small group.

"That seems an awfully long way," said the General's wife. She did not acknowledge her husband's arrival.

"About the same distance from London to Bombay, in fact."

"So it would take five days to get up there? That would be wearisome, without even a change of scenery or stopovers."

"Oh, not at all."

Maxwell Spencer was getting warmed up with his subject and given half a chance would talk all evening. Maliha had experienced the same effect when she had been cornered by Valerie, and made the mistake of mentioning she had never read an Indian romance by Bithia Mary Croker. She had come away reeling from the onslaught of plot details and character names.

"You see this top-of-the-range sky liner—the pride of the P&O fleet— has a maximum speed of a mere 100 miles per hour. But a vessel built to travel the void, even one that only travels between the ground and the station, can achieve speeds of *500 miles per hour* or even more: Less than a day is required to reach the station."

"And you will be going up?" asked Mrs Makepeace-Flynn innocently. There was no doubt she already knew the answer and sought only to pierce his good humour.

There was a distinct lag in Maxwell's enthusiasm. "Not personally, no."

The General chose that moment to cut in. "Evening, Barbara. Max. Seen Lochana by any chance?"

If Mrs Makepeace-Flynn's tone with Maxwell Spencer had been subtly cutting, her response to her husband was undisguised malice.

"I have not. Perhaps she fell overboard."

Valerie Spencer chose that moment to turn away and take a long sip from her glass. Her husband, on the other hand, completely failed to recognise the menace.

"Oh, nobody can actually fall overboard, can they? I mean the upper decks are fully enclosed and do not open."

"Who's fallen overboard?" Temperance arrived from deeper within the lounge; a freshly lit cigarette burned in the holder dangling from her left hand; she wore a very modern dress with a distinctly French look about it and no corset. Mrs Makepeace-Flynn's face reddened with the effrontery of such a provocative garment, and even Valerie looked shocked. The General seemed unmoved.

"Seen my nurse, Miss Williams?"

Temperance looked down at the General as if he had just crawled out of a sewer. Then her face relaxed, she placed the tip of her cigarette holder delicately between her lips and drew a leisurely breath.

"She came through the lounge earlier, said she was feeling a little under the weather. She said she might take a turn about the Promenade deck."

"Oh dear, she's not well?" Valerie chimed in. "Perhaps someone should check on her." And her eyes flew to Maliha. "Don't you think so, Miss Anderson?"

Maliha smiled, one thing you could be sure of with Valerie Spencer, she would never use Maliha's first name. "I'm sure I wouldn't know, Valerie, besides who would push the General?"

"Quite right," said the General. On cue, the dinner gong sounded and like Pavlovian dogs the ensemble drifted towards the companionway. "If you wouldn't mind, Maliha."

iii

The dining salon's round tables had been transformed. Where they had the simple adornments for tea earlier in the afternoon, they now carried a ravishing selection of crockery and cutlery. There were huge flower arrangements that towered thin and spindly up to the ceiling with a minimum of support. Elegant glassware—made especially for the vessel—with images from Greek mythology engraved into them, artistry of the finest quality, finished off the place settings in fine style. Rows of Greco-Roman columns supported the ceiling and the walls were decorated with Greek frescoes. During the day, the pictures were covered up using curtains, to give the room a cosier aspect.

Being forward of the main cabin areas the port side was lined with windows that looked out on the darkening sky and the Red Sea; they were now travelling south-east along the African coast, when they reached Abyssinia they would turn north-east following the Gulf of Aden and thence to the Indian Ocean and Bombay.

Stewards moved swiftly but without haste, seating travellers in the oak chairs and providing drinks as needed. Maliha wheeled the General into position as one of the stewards removed a heavy chair from the table, then she took her place between him and Maxwell Spencer.

Each person at the table positioned themselves in their usual configuration. There was a vacant seat on the other side of the General that would have been occupied by Lochana and beyond that Mrs Makepeace-Flynn. Beside her on the other side was James Crier, a banker or accountant, Maliha wasn't sure which. He disconcerted her in that he did not express the natural prejudice of his peers, and always took time to be interested in his companions—an interest that seemed quite genuine.

The General's wife had taken to him and apparently he never tired of listening to her complaints. Continuing clockwise around the table, there was Temperance who was another confusing character: she was passionate in her faith but fond of Parisian fashion. She had been very friendly towards Maliha on the first day but turned cold quite quickly. After which she had turned her attentions to Lochana.

Then came Valerie Spencer and finally Maxwell. It was easy to prod Maxwell into talking for a long time before he wound down and to Maliha, at least, his talk of machines and engineering were not uninteresting even if he did have a habit of repeating himself. As a result, the evening meals were not as arduous as they might have been. If Maxwell dried up or conversed with his wife, the General was another easy target for a pretence of conversation.

Apparently Mr Crier had commented about war wounds and set off the General.

"Not been bound to this damn chair for very long at all. Last saw action in the Transvaal, putting down that damn farmer's revolt back in '02."

Temperance's head jerked up. "But surely, General, it was their land."

"Nonsense. We took it fair and square back in the 80s; they only existed at all under our sufferance. We let them stay, and farm, provided protection from the natives, then they had the audacity to object."

Temperance looked down at her plate. "You just don't see it, do you? You started with the Welsh, then the Scots, then anywhere else in the world that isn't significant enough to give you pause. A nation of bullies." Her accent became more pronounced with every word.

"Oh look, the first course!" broke in Valerie, as waiters flooded from the door at the end of the salon. "I wonder what it is."

"Fish," said Mr Crier.

Maliha breathed a quiet sigh of relief and turned her attention towards the food.

iv

The General's nurse failed to put in an appearance during dinner and, as a consequence, Maliha was co-opted for more wheelchair management. They returned to the lounge for Bridge. The tradition of the men drinking and smoking without the ladies was dispensed with on-board and, as the evening drew on, it was natural to either retire or return to the lounge. The Spencers had chosen to retire, claiming the shortened days of the vessel for their excuse.

Maliha found herself the General's partner against Temperance and Mrs Makepeace-Flynn. The other tables were filled with games of whist and backgammon. The electric lights burned through the pall of smoke that rose from the combined combustion of a hundred cigars, pipes and cigarettes. The steady hum of conversation filled the ears with the occasional bark of laughter or raised voice.

While through the wide expanse of glass in the stern, the twin trails of smoke were lit by a brilliant moon that reflected off the Red Sea with the dark masses of Africa to the left and Araby to the right.

It was all so civilised. So British.

Both Mrs Makepeace-Flynn and Temperance were matched in their aggressive bidding and more often than not, one or other was dummy forcing Maliha to remain at the table. But the General was more measured, though it might have been the brandy slowing him down. Maliha bid predictably, she had learned years ago it did not pay to stand out. At around 10pm, they were on the last hand of a rubber, and she was dummy.

She grabbed at the opportunity and excused herself for the night. A turn around the deck to clear her head of the smoke and noise seemed wise, and she quickly mounted the stairs, she kept on past the Promenade deck up to the Observation deck. As she had expected there were many passengers of a similar mind, but the subdued lighting protected her from their stares.

She looked over the inner balcony down on to the Promenade deck. Some young fellows were playing football with their jackets for goalposts. It was a foolish idea in reduced gravity, but their good-humoured laughter at their own antics, bouncing high into the air and doing somersaults, and making the ball fly to prodigious heights and distances made her smile; although she judged them a little worse for drink.

Moving to the outer hull, she gazed into the dark. The moon's light sparkled on both the rotors and the sea. Here and there, along the coastline, the light of fires; perhaps tribes of African nomads, or villages of sun-baked mud buildings.

v

"A penny for your thoughts, Miss Anderson?"

"Mr Crier." He had appeared beside her, quiet as a mouse. He held a glass of wine in one hand and a glass of water in the other. He proffered the water to her.

"I know you don't drink alcohol."

"Thank you." She took a sip, ice clinked across the surface, and the ripples sloshed in the slow way they did under reduced gravity. He turned away from her and stared out across the dark landscape, and up at the moon.

"Like a jewel hung in ghastly night, makes black night beauteous and her old face new." He said. Maliha took another hurried sip and wondered if she should leave; that was a rather racy sonnet of the Bard's. "Oh, I do apologise, Miss Anderson, I really was talking about the moon. Perhaps you would prefer me to withdraw?"

"No. It is fine, really."

He took a deep breath and sipped his wine. "It seems a shame we should have to travel without being able to breathe the fresh air, don't you think?"

"You could travel by boat."

"I think that might be pleasant, but everyone is such a hurry nowadays, and all the quality liners are in the sky. To travel by boat would mean a great reduction in luxury."

"I do not think you would be forced to scrub the decks."

He laughed. "No, perhaps not. But one does enjoy the trappings of first class. And the company can be most pleasing."

"Sometimes, it can."

"Perhaps if we were on a coastal scow you would not be forced to replace a missing nurse and not even get paid for the duty."

The term *duty* conjured other images in Maliha's mind to those intended. "I don't mind."

He turned to face her. She felt uncomfortable beneath his gaze. "Perhaps you should."

"It is not my nature, Mr Crier." She hid behind another sip and the cold water slid across her tongue. "It is not done." The words were placatory, but her tone was strained.

"There," he said. "I believe you are a suffragist."

"You may believe what you wish," she said. "Thank you for the water. I believe I shall retire now."

As she walked away in long, careful strides, she felt as if his eyes burned into her back. She cursed herself for reacting to him. Clearly he was playing some game, he had sought her out, evidenced by the glass of water; deliberately engaged her in conversation and then goaded her into reaction. It was all very inappropriate.

vi

Lochana Modi opened her eyes. Her head throbbed in a way that made even looking painful. The cabin she was in was almost complete shadow, just a hint of moonlight. She attempted to rise and instantly clutched at her lower ribs as an agonising stabbing pain ripped through her, she slumped back breathing heavily with a gurgling catch in her throat.

Her bodice was sodden, and her fingers wet with whatever the thick gooey liquid was. She stretched out her arm and stared at the dripping dark that covered the palm of her hand. Then she knew and tears filled up her eyes.

It was so unfair. All she ever offered anyone was love.

Cold seeped through her, eating at her. Already her feet were like ice.

"No." She had meant the word to scare away Death as it came for her. But though the sound came from her mouth she barely heard it above the wheezing. Whimpering with the pain she took hold of the sofa's arm and levered herself to her feet. She staggered for a moment as she found her balance. Her head swam. Her training told her that she had lost a lot of blood.

She had seen men die. She did not want to die. If only she could get help.

She took an uncertain step towards the door.

CHAPTER 3

It was morning. The sun poured through the windows of the dining salon. Maliha sat alone at breakfast at a small table near the inner wall. The tables near the windows were filled with other passengers. The Spencers had nabbed their own, and Mr Crier was eating with some people she recognised but had never spoken with. The General and his wife were at another. Maliha frowned; this was the first morning Lochana had not been in attendance. Perhaps she really was ill, as Temperance had suggested.

There was no one in first class who would consider checking on her, and it would be inappropriate to approach the General and ask him, especially with what she had observed and Mrs Makepeace-Flynn's undisguised animosity. No, that was not a discussion to engage in. It would be best if she simply visited Lochana's cabin.

She took a final sip of coffee; it was a vice, but one could not be completely pure in the real world. Besides the scent of fresh ground coffee was a form of beauty and there was no point grinding coffee only for the smell.

She left the table and headed out through the double doors into the main companionway. It took only a few minutes to traverse the distance to the cabins. She composed herself and knocked lightly. She waited a few moments then knocked a little harder.

She waited again, a feeling of concern rose within her. She knocked firmly, and more times than would be considered proper. A response was not forthcoming. She tried the door handle, but it was locked. She turned from the door intending to find a steward and alert them to the situation when something else caught her attention.

The sound of the engines and their vibrations had changed.

Maliha ran to the window. The ship was not due to touch down until they reached Bombay in the late evening, around eleven o'clock. The blueness of the Gulf of Aden stretched out to the horizon with not even an island in sight. But the central rotor was turning to the vertical position. She pressed her face to the glass, peering forward and then to the stern. The other rotors were also turning.

It was impossible to see what was happening from here.

She headed back to the main companionway. She had expected to see hordes of people flooding from the salon and rushing up on deck. But the companionway was nearly empty from end to end, a couple of stewards moving in the lounge to the stern and another she didn't recognise moving towards the salon for their breakfast.

She took the stairs to the Observation deck. She thought she could perceive the difference in the way the ship vibrated as the rotors would be fully vertical now. The ship would be drifting forwards with its thousands of tons of momentum. The Captain had not issued orders for reverse thrust which would have been very noticeable so she could only assume the change had nothing to do with anything down on the surface. It had to do with the sky liner itself.

She burst from the door out on to the deck; the sun beat down through the dome from the front, but Maliha's attention was immediately grabbed by the passengers spread out along the outer rail, peering down. She moved towards them. They were most closely pressed together near the stern where the windows came to an end. She could only join the group after the last person standing in line with the central rotor.

Being careful not to touch the man who stood at the furthermost position, she stretched out across the rail and attempted to make out what they were looking at. Unfortunately, the man was quite large and he too was stretching to see around the crowd to his left.

Maliha sighed quietly. This was not the first time she'd had this sort of problem though, on previous occasions, those blocking her had been doing it deliberately. At least it wasn't malicious on this occasion. There was nothing for it but to step up onto the railing. There was no danger to life, the wall of glass and steel prevented anyone from falling overboard; the only risk was to her pride, and she had little enough of that. And not one iota to lose to the other passengers.

She lifted her skirt and placed her boot on the lowest metal rail then hauled herself up with a slight twinge from her injured thigh, but that passed quickly. She sat on the rail and leaned out, pressing her outstretched hand against the cold glass for support. She looked down.

The most immediate impression she got was that there was now nothing between her and a drop of 3,000ft to the sea below. Then her attention was taken by events in the side of the vessel. A hatch had been opened in the hull above the rear wing below the level of the rotor.

A platform had been run out, and three sailors stood half in, and half out holding a rope as another crew member climbed down rungs set into the hull. At intervals, he ran his rope through attachments mounted parallel to the rungs: A wise precaution as the down-draught from the rotor whipped his hair and clothes like a gale. She noted he had a second, much thinner, rope being paid out as he descended. A second man with a stout rope about his waist exited the hatch and followed the first down.

The rear rotor itself was running perfectly smoothly as far as she could tell and he did not appear to have any tools; she wondered what he could be doing. It was then she saw it, flapping and fluttering under the rotor's gusting power, a collection of rags caught on the rear wing. Then she let out a gasp as she saw a hand moving, and the randomness of the air flows lifted the rags revealing a slim body before hiding it again in the next moment.

Maliha stared in morbid fascination as the crewman reached the curved surface of the wing and stood under the battering force of the rotor. He attached the rope to another hook embedded into the metal then took measured steps across to where the tangled clothing continued to flap about. Kneeling beside the body, he took a few moments to examine it then pulled on the second rope.

A stretcher was passed out from the hatch just as the second crewman made it to the wing; he reached the body and helped the first crewman guide the stretcher as it was buffeted back and forth in the wind. Once on the surface of the wing they lashed it down and proceeded to disentangle the body from where it was caught. They transferred it to the stretcher and strapped the arms, body and legs.

At their signal the rope attached to the stretcher tightened, and it rose from the wing. Holding their end of the rope tight, they managed to get the stretcher up to the hatch without bumping it against the hull too many times. The stretcher was brought inboard. But in those last moments Maliha had seen everything she needed to see. It was Lochana Modi. Dead.

ii

Maliha stepped down awkwardly from the rail, surprised to see the much bigger crowd that now surrounded her. Directly in front of her a man pushed past her as soon as she'd vacated the space by the rail. He didn't even look at her. But with the recovery of the body the crowd broke apart. Only those wanting to watch to the bitter end continued to hang over the edge.

The low buzz of conversation grew steadily as those who had not been able to see were told the events by those who had. Maliha pushed through the crowd as carefully as she could. She needed to get to the Purser, the only member of the senior crew that a passenger could easily contact.

Under ordinary circumstances, she would have avoided the crowded stairs that led from the Observation deck down to the Promenade, but this was no time to worry about such things. She pushed her way through the crowd and joined the queue of passengers heading down. There was barely a glance in her direction.

A jumble of thoughts pressed in on her. How could Lochana's body be outside the hull? If she hadn't become caught on the wing, she would simply have disappeared without a trace into the sea. Temperance had seen her in the lounge sometime between six and seven, so she had been alive then. But seemingly no one had seen her afterwards. Could she have fallen from the Promenade deck? That seemed impossible: there were no opening windows on either of the open public decks.

Maliha crossed the Promenade deck heading forward to where the Purser's office was accessible from the passenger deck and the ship's superstructure.

The cabin windows had catches which were soldered to prevent tampering. They could be opened but with difficulty. Lochana's cabin was inboard and had no windows, but she did have access to the General's cabin, so if she had been able to open the window there she could have fallen that way. But would she have taken her own life?

Maliha pushed open the door into the Purser's outer office. A large oak desk acted as a barrier across the cabin. A crewman of Indian origin and unhappy demeanour stood at a filing cabinet replacing a folder. He looked round as she entered.

"I must speak to the Purser immediately."

The man smiled. "I am afraid he is unavailable at present, Miss Anderson."

Maliha was impressed though she could appreciate the benefits of knowing all of the ship's first class passengers by sight. They could be very difficult. "I expect he is dealing with the body you found on the wing."

"A most unfortunate affair."

"Yes, of course, but I know who she is."

He became serious. "You know?"

"It's General Makepeace-Flynn's nurse: Lochana Modi."

He picked up the phone on the desk, consulted a chart of dialling codes next to the phone and dialled a four digit number.

"It is the Assistant Purser here … Yes … Is the Purser available? … Yes, quite important … Yes, sir. I have one of the passengers here. She says she knows who the body is … Lochana Modi, General Makepeace-Flynn's nurse … Miss Maliha Anderson … yes, sir. Very good."

He slowly placed the phone back in its cradle.

"Would you mind waiting?" He indicated a row of hard-backed wooden chairs upholstered in green leather. Maliha took a seat. She felt the vibrations in the ship changing again and surmised they were underway once more. She glanced at the two clocks on the wall. One showed the time in London while the other was local time. They were now three hours ahead. She adjusted her watch; they had already gained an hour on Constantinople and Khartoum.

iii

The ship's doctor, in leather apron and with his shirt sleeves rolled up, examined the body of the woman. The examination room was crowded with the Captain, Purser, Master-at-Arms, as well as the doctor's assistant and the ratings who had brought the body on board.

The death would not look good on his record, thought the Captain. Fifteen years as the master of passenger vessels, ten years in the Royal Navy before that and never anything like this.

The doctor cut away the tattered remains of the outer clothing, enough to examine the body. The skin was covered in pink splotches with a network of scrapes and abrasions across the entire surface.

The Purser excused himself.

"All this damage is post-mortem," the Doctor said to the unasked question. "Rigor mortis is setting in now."

The MAA looked interested. "So she was killed this morning?"

"Can't say, there's no rigor at low temperatures, she could have been out there all night."

"So when?"

"Hypostasis—the blotches—suggests all night but there's no distinct pooling, she was moving around the whole time by the looks of it." He looked up at the Captain. "It's a miracle we found her at all. If she hadn't got caught she'd have been gone and you'd just have had a missing person."

"Can't say that would have been worse," said the Captain. "Any idea how she died?"

The Doctor smiled. "That's the easy bit. Here." He pointed to a spot just below the ribs on the left of the body where an inch-long ragged hole broke the skin. The Doctor prodded and looked inside with a small electric torch. "The blade was probably about six to eight inches long, quite thick too. Whoever did it certainly made an effort to cause damage: made a right mess of the liver. She would have taken a while to die though. Very painful."

"Are you saying she was murdered?"

"Unless she accidentally fell on the blade then wriggled about a lot before getting off and throwing herself out of the window. No? It was murder."

The Captain sighed and turned to the Master-at-Arms while the doctor attacked the remainder of the clothes. "Alright, you'd better start an investigation."

"This is a little outside my experience, sir."

"None of us is going to come out of this looking good, Chief. If we can sort it out before we hit Bombay—"

"Oh, dear god." The doctor's voice was a complete change from his previous blasé attitude. The others stared at him. "Lochana Modi was not a woman."

The MAA spluttered. "Are you sure?"

"It is a fairly fundamental factor in medical training but if you doubt me feel free to take a look at him yourself. I'm sure you're familiar with the basics."

iv

The cabin door was pushed open by a large man with a ruddy complexion and a handlebar moustache. Along with his height and girth it gave him a commanding aspect, and he knew it. Maliha did not know who he was beyond the fact he wore a uniform and was not the Purser. She resolved not to be intimidated as he came to a shuddering halt before the desk. The Assistant Purser glanced purposefully in her direction. He turned and loomed over her.

"Miss Anderson." He thrust out his hand. She was uncertain whether he intended to shake, or pull her from her seat. She stood and placed her hand in his. It disappeared but his skin was soft and he did no more than squeeze gently. "Please come into the office."

The Assistant already had the door open and, having seated Maliha opposite the officer's chair, closed it gently after them.

"I am the Master-at-Arms, Charles Grey. You may refer to me as Mr Grey. I am dealing with the current situation." He stared at Maliha for a moment, as if seeing her for the first time. It was a look she had seen many times before. It came with the cognisance that the person in front of them was not as white as the viewer had previously thought. "Would you like some tea?"

"No, thank you," she said. "Perhaps we should get to the point?"

He nodded and looked down at the desk. He scanned it and, failing to find what he was looking for, opened a drawer from which he extracted a number of sheets of paper with rows and lined columns. Something for accounts, she thought. He took a pen from the rack and wrote her name at the top, the date and the two times which he took his two wristwatches.

"I am investigating the death of a passenger."

"Yes."

"I understand you have some relevant information?"

"Did they not tell you?"

"I would rather hear it first-hand."

"Alright. The woman you recovered from outside, it's Lochana Modi. She came onboard with the General. She's his nurse."

"Is she?"

Maliha frowned. "Yes, of course."

- 27 -

The MAA stared down at his piece of paper. "And you know this because?"

"Because I have spoken to her. I have played cards with her. I have seen her with the General."

"No doubt. But how do you know the body was—" he hesitated for a moment. "—her?"

"I was watching from the Observation deck. She was wearing the same clothes as yesterday. And I saw her face, although it was a fair way away."

"The clothes were badly torn. The face was ... damaged."

"Yes, but I had seen her in the afternoon, I was in the stern lounge when she came back on board with Temperance Williams. She was wearing the same clothes." Which was odd now she came to think of it, why had Lochana not changed after the heat of Khartoum?

"You saw her?"

"I was in the lounge watching for them because it was getting late. I did not know if they had adjusted their watches. The General was there too." Maliha grasped what was behind his words. "She was murdered."

The MAA's head jerked up. "No one said anything about murder."

"And you're thinking I might have done it," she said. "What possible reason could I have?"

"The number of possible suspects is very limited, Miss Anderson."

"About five hundred, I would have thought."

"Not everyone would have a motive, Miss Anderson. I'm sure we can limit it to those who have had regular contact with the victim."

"And I have a motive, do I?"

"You admit yourself you spend a great deal of time with the General. Perhaps you would like to take the place of," again the curious hesitation. "Miss Modi."

Something exploded inside Maliha. It was not the Master-At-Arms himself. It was not the fact that he considered her a suspect. It was all the times in her life that the finger had been pointed in her direction because she was different.

"Have you the slightest idea who my parents are? Do you even care?" Maliha found herself on her feet, shouting at the seated man. "I do not require a job. And if I did I believe I could do somewhat better than a position tending the General and putting up with the constant sniping from his jealous wife. If you want someone to suspect, perhaps you should look a little closer to home."

Her hands were shaking. She could feel tears in her eyes as the anger overcame her; anger from so many years of lies and hatred. She turned on her heel, pulled the door open and stormed through, finding herself floating a little too high and long she impacted the wall opposite. Inside she screamed. She could not even manage an elegant exit.

When she finally managed to get out on to the deck, the tears were flowing down her cheeks. People were looking at her. She turned away and faced the glass wall, looking out across the sea though she could barely make out where sea ended and the sky began through the tears. She clicked open her reticule and rummaged for a kerchief.

Something white appeared in front of her.

"Here, *cariad*." The soft tone of Temperance Williams penetrated her suppressed anger. She took the kerchief, dabbed at her cheeks and sniffed.

"Sorry." She offered the damp cloth back to Temperance.

"Keep it." Maliha felt a hand grip her elbow, turning and pushing her towards the stern. "Let's go somewhere more private."

v

Temperance Williams' cabin was of a similar layout and decoration to Maliha's, but was one of the cheaper inboard ones. It lacked a rug, had fewer cushions and less china adorning the walls. The sofa where she sat had an elegant Turkish cloth thrown over it which Maliha recognised as an item Temperance had bought in Constantinople.

Daylight spilled into the room through a small lace covered window opening onto the companionway which in turn had windows at its end. The room was lit by electric lights situated around the walls. Temperance had ordered some tea and served it when the maid had left.

"Now," said Temperance. "What has happened?"

Maliha stared down into her tea. "Lochana is dead. Murdered."

"I don't understand."

"The fuss this morning, when the ship stopped they were recovering her body."

"Recovering her body? From where?"

"Outside, on one of the wings."

Temperance sipped her tea thoughtfully. "Why were you crying, *cariad?*"

"I was being interviewed by the Master-at-Arms. He said I was a suspect."

Maliha was shocked from her introspection by the sudden barking laugh from Temperance. "How utterly ridiculous. Anyone who knew you would know you are far too decent a human being to do such a thing."

"That's very kind, Temperance. However I'm sure anyone is capable of any act given the right motivation or the right set of circumstances." Unconsciously she rubbed the ridged scar on her thigh. "One does not always consider the consequences when one is in the grip of emotion."

They went quiet and drank their tea.

At length Temperance placed her cup down with a solid clink into its saucer. "So, Miss Anderson," she said. "What do you intend to do about it?"

"I don't know what you mean."

"You have been falsely accused."

"I'm only a suspect," she said. "Using their criteria you would also be one."

"What about Valerie, Max and that Mr Crier? Oh, and the delightful Mrs Makepeace-Flynn."

"Yes, of course, perhaps some of the crew as well."

"So which is it?"

"I couldn't say." Maliha wished Temperance would drop the subject but she refused to let go.

"Let's just review what we know, shall we? Why don't you tell me what you said to the Master-at-Arms?"

"I said I didn't know a great deal. I saw you come back from Khartoum with her. That you mentioned you'd seen her between six and seven, I suppose the times would really be six and quarter of seven because that's when we turned up."

"I think it was shortly after six."

"Yes, and she told you she wasn't coming to dinner."

"And that's it?"

"That's all, I said."

Temperance looked at her watch. "We have a couple of hours until lunch. What say we have a snoop around and see what we can find?"

CHAPTER 4

i

Maliha trailed Temperance as she strode down the main companionway. People stood around in small groups speaking quietly with worried voices. The news of the death was now common knowledge and even the word murder was uttered. Maliha considered how impossible it was to keep a secret like this. They turned into the passage that led past Maliha's cabin to Lochana's and the General's.

A crewman stood outside Lochana's door. He had a gun holstered at his side. Maliha hesitated, but Temperance did not even pause. She approached the sailor, and Maliha could not fail to notice the way he took in Temperance's slim modern form.

"Can I help, Miss?" he said.

"Oh dear," said Temperance in such a soft voice that Maliha studied her face carefully to make sure she was not unwell. The woman that stood so tall and proud at all times was transformed into some meek child. She clasped her hands demurely at waist height and did not make eye contact. Clearly Temperance had missed her calling on the stage. "I'm really sorry..."

"What's the problem, Miss?"

Temperance hesitated. "This is all so awkward and so sad. I really hope you can help."

"Whatever I can do, Miss."

"It's so terrible, Miss Modi..." Temperance pulled out a kerchief and dabbed at her eyes. "But, oh, this is too awful."

"Should I fetch someone?" This time he addressed his comments to Maliha and noticed her for the first time. He looked back at Temperance.

"No, I need to fetch my Bible."

"Your Bible?"

"I feel so foolish. I lent my very own family Bible to Miss Modi. You see I am taking up a position as a missionary to the Hindu ladies of India. I was instructing Miss Modi on the wonder of God's Grace. I lent her my very own family Bible. And now this..."

"Shall I fetch it out for you?"

Temperance laid her hand gently on his arm and looked up into his eyes. "Oh no, I could not ask you to leave your post. We can find it as quick as may be." She smiled at him.

ii

The door closed behind them, and Maliha switched on the electric light. Temperance regained her usual poise. "Men are pathetic."

The room was another inboard cabin without windows. In this case, it was specifically intended as servants' quarters and had a connecting door to a large cabin on the outside. The wooden floor had a rug in front of the sofa, and the armchair while off to the side was the writing desk near the connecting door to the master cabin.

Something nagged at Maliha. She stared around the room again frowning.

"Problem?" asked Temperance. As she spoke, raised male voices filtered through to them. The door slammed open, and the Master-At-Arms stormed in.

Temperance shrank back to become the mouse version of herself. But the MAA's attention and anger was not directed at her. His ire was reserved solely and entirely for Maliha.

"What's the meaning of this? Tampering with evidence, Miss Anderson?"

Maliha stood her ground, but her thoughts were not coherent. She knew she should be paying attention to the Master-At-Arms, but there was something in the room that was just not right. Temperance came to her aid.

"Oh no, sir. It is my fault."

His eyes did not leave Maliha. "And you are?"

"Temperance Williams. Missionary."

"Really."

Maliha frowned again and turned away from the Master-At-Arms. She studied the sofa and, with a feeling of relief, saw the thing that troubled her.

"That end cushion is upside-down, Mr Grey," she said and pointed at the left-hand end. The sofa was of the three seat variety, with individual cushions for each position. The cushions were shaped so that each end one was an L-shaped piece that fitted around the front of the armrest. Each was

- 32 -

patterned and when observed more closely it was clear the pattern of the left-hand cushion did not match.

The Master-At-Arms made a harrumphing sound. "What's that got to do with anything?"

Maliha, feeling more confident, turned back and met his gaze. "What reason might you have for turning a cushion over in a murdered woman's room?"

The man was not a fool. Two strides took him to the erroneous cushion, and he flipped it over. A mottled brown stain covered most of the surface.

"So this is where she was murdered," said Temperance.

He looked at her. "Of course not."

It was the turn of Temperance to look confused. "Why not?"

"Look around, Miss Williams."

Temperance did not look, but her eyes narrowed, and she opened her mouth for a sharp retort. Maliha interrupted before she could say anything. "There are no other bloodstains and besides, how did she get outside?" She said the words but her mind was already racing ahead because there was still something wrong with the sofa, and now she knew what it was. "Anyhow, that cushion doesn't belong in here."

The MAA looked down at the cushion in his hands and back at her. "How could you possibly know that? We use the same design throughout this deck."

Maliha knew that thoughts of her guilt were running through his mind again. It was very tiresome. "I did not kill her."

"That remains to be seen. How can you possibly suggest this cushion does not belong in this room?"

"Try putting it back the right way up." Maliha said dismissively. She turned away from him and went to the connecting door to the General's room. She turned the handle and pulled, but the door did not move.

The MAA swore in a most indelicate way. "It's a right-hand end cushion."

Temperance laughed. "There you are. Mr Grey, is it? No woman would make such a mistake."

Maliha took a piece of paper from the writing desk and slid it into the top of the gap between the door and the frame. She carefully slid it down until it reached the handle level where it met an obstruction. "It's bolted on that side. I wonder why?" She turned to where both of them were staring at her.

"Why shouldn't it be bolted?" asked Temperance.

Maliha hesitated. The secret moment between the General and Lochana that she had observed was almost a precious trust. But if it helped to find Lochana's murderer it would be best to reveal all the truth. But what of any embarrassment to the General's wife? No, Maliha was sure Mrs Makepeace-Flynn already knew. It was the only thing that explained her attitude.

"Because I believe the General and Lochana were—" she paused and gathered her courage. "—intimate."

Despite everything, she was not prepared for the surprise that took hold of Mr Grey's face, which rapidly degenerated into utter disgust. Temperance had only a look of disgust.

"That is a very serious accusation, young lady." The words seem to have been torn from the MAA's gut. Maliha felt a twinge of anger that he should be disgusted at a liaison between an Englishman and Indian woman. After all that described her parents precisely.

"There you are," said Temperance. "Must have been the General."

iii

The Captain's day cabin was equipped with various tables, chairs and desks; there was a wide sofa along one wall over which hung photographs of various ships of the Royal Navy. There were no windows. Captain Jones stood at ease behind his desk as the steward pushed open the door from the companionway with his elbow and then backed in pulling the General in his wheelchair. As the door swung back, the steward turned the General round and pushed him into position opposite the Captain.

The Captain moved round the desk and shook the General's hand. The man looked grey and feeble, as if all the blood had been drained from him. His hand was cold, and it was like clasping a withered leaf. The old soldier put no effort into the formality. Captain Jones nodded at the steward and the man left.

It was a very awkward situation thought the Captain as he took his seat opposite the man. It was hard to think that this was the same irritating gentleman that had come aboard four days earlier.

"Would you like a drink, General?" The General shook his head; staring at the desk in front of him, but the Captain was certain the man saw only his inner thoughts. "A cigar?"

"Say what you must say."

The question on the Captain's mind was not one he could say outright. It was the kind of question that must be approached sideways. There were easier questions.

"I must, of course, ask about the death of your nurse."

The General did not respond.

"When did you see Lochana Modi last?"

The General took a deep breath. "It was in the afternoon between three and four o'clock." He finally looked up and met the Captain's eye. "I did not kill Lochana, Captain."

"The ship's doctor says she died in the evening, most likely, but he was unable to specify the time with any degree of precision."

"The last time we spoke was in the afternoon."

"Can you tell me the nature of the discussion you had?"

"I do not recall," he said. "Do you have a nip of whiskey?"

The Captain took a few moments to pour a drink from his private stock. It was a decent single malt. General Makepeace-Flynn took the glass and cradled it for a few moments before taking a sip. The Captain resumed his seat and leaned forward across the desk.

"There is a steward who was on duty at that time who will swear that you spoke with raised voices."

"Yes, alright. I was angry with the amount of time Lochana was spending in the company of Miss Williams."

"Miss Williams?"

"Some Welsh missionary travelling first class, if you please. Full of zeal which she decided to expend on my nurse." The emotion he expected from the General was creeping back.

"So if you did not kill your nurse, General, who did?"

"I don't know! And let me tell you that if I did then I would be doing your job for you and that person would pay!"

"She's just a nurse, General. Just a native."

"You, sir, are a fool!" The General looked very much as if he wanted to pull himself from the chair and wrap his fingers around the Captain's neck.

"But Lochana Modi was not a woman at all, was she? He was a man."

The General slumped back into his wheelchair and looked, for all the world, as if he were going to cry. The Captain hoped he would not.

iv

Maliha and Temperance waited outside the General's cabin. Mr Grey had not allowed them to enter though he left the door open, perhaps hoping for some insight from Maliha. The view it afforded them was better than nothing. It was quickly confirmed the right-hand cushion of the General's sofa was also the wrong one and presumably the one swapped. But as the MAA continued his search Maliha became disinterested. He was looking in all the wrong places.

Without a word she turned away, went to the nearest window and looked out. It confirmed what she already thought; all the cabins on this companionway were forward of the rear wing.

She judged that anything thrown from her own window would be eaten by the rotor as her cabin was slightly forward of it, but the General's cabin was further toward the stern and thus behind the rotor. From his windows, an object would be caught in its air stream, blown backwards, and probably lost forever. Unless, by some happenstance, it was a heavy object that managed to fall onto the wing and get caught on some protuberance before being thrown into oblivion.

"What are you doing?" said Temperance from the door.

"Just thinking."

"I am told gentlemen are not attracted to women who think."

Maliha looked at Temperance in her Parisian dress. "It's not something that concerns me."

The lunch gong sounded, echoing down the passageways.

"Oh good, all this sleuthing has made me quite ravenous," said Temperance. "Shall we?" She put her arm out for Maliha to slip hers through and smiled. Dutifully Maliha did so while hiding her reluctance, and allowed herself to be led through the ship to the dining salon.

Friendship was a concept she understood in principle but since leaving India and all her real friends at age eleven, it was not something she had experienced. She had soon learned that any friendship offered at the school was always a mask for betrayal. She found it hard to imagine that

Temperance's offer of camaraderie was honest, though she had no sensible reason to doubt it.

There were fewer people in the salon than usual. Those who knew they were not the perpetrator considered themselves potential victims. Rationality did not come into it.

The table was set with melon. Maliha sat in her usual seat. The place to her left where the General would normally have sat contained a chair and an untouched place setting, likewise the next seat which would have been Lochana's. Mrs Makepeace-Flynn sat in her place with Temperance beside her. Maliha was somewhat surprised since that would normally have been where Mr Crier sat; he was one place further along. Max and Valerie were not in their places. Maliha was on her own.

Mr Crier stood up. "Miss Anderson, would you consider it inappropriate for me to sit next to you; otherwise there will be no one for you to talk to."

Maliha did consider it inappropriate and had a great deal to think about, but those were not words she could say. "You are very thoughtful, Mr Crier."

Which is how she found herself having luncheon with a man. He dug his spoon into the melon. Waiters drifted in and removed the food from the other settings.

"A most unpleasant business," he said.

"Yes."

"Do you have an opinion on it?"

"I see no value in having an opinion, Mr Crier. This is not art, it is murder." She punctuated her comment by cutting into the melon with her spoon and taking a mouthful. A dribble of juice escaped her lips and she hurriedly dabbed it with her napkin. One benefit of reduced gravity was that dribbles travelled at a very unhurried pace which meant it was easy to catch them before they became too obvious.

"I understand you are travelling home."

"That is correct."

"Do you disembark this evening?"

"No, at the Fortress in Ceylon. Then I take a flier to Puducherry and a carriage home." She concentrated on the melon, but the outer skin was soon stripped clean. The plates were cleared without a fuss and replaced with plates of various sandwiches, cheeses and light biscuits.

"You attended Roedean I believe, Miss Anderson."

The sandwich she was lifting to her mouth came to an abrupt stop. He knew. This was really too much. Was there nowhere she could go to escape the notoriety? She felt the scar on her leg begin to itch. She frowned in annoyance.

She set down her sandwich and looked across at Temperance who had her lips very close to Mrs Makepeace-Flynn's ear and was whispering something with a look of self-righteous pride on her face. On hearing the words, the General's wife's face distorted into a mask of complex emotions that were hard to fathom. But there was pain and anger in there, perhaps hatred and loathing too.

There was a commotion at the main entrance to the salon. Maliha was forced to turn in her chair to see. The General had been pushed through the doors by a steward, who had managed to make a meal of it, scraping the wheel against the wood of the door. Maliha noted the shell of a military uniform that encased the pale wasted figure the General had become. She barely noticed Mrs Makepeace-Flynn getting up from her chair.

Maliha watched long enough to see the General's wife approach her husband raise her arm and slap him with all her strength. An act to which he did not react. She then strode from the room, head high. Maliha turned back in her chair and saw the faces of all the diners watching the event. Including Temperance, her lips pressed into a thin humourless smile.

v

The General dismissed the steward and locked himself in. He glanced at the connecting door to Lochana's room. He rolled himself to the drinks cabinet and poured a large whiskey. He held the glass between his knees and pushed himself over to the writing desk.

He took a sheet of paper and the steel-nibbed pen his wife had given him for his 50th birthday, the finest pen produced from the Birmingham factories. He unscrewed the ink pot and charged the reservoir. Now his secret was known to so many, the ignominy would be too difficult for his wife to endure. And the law would not be far behind.

It did not take long to write what he needed to say. He pressed the upturned sheet into the blotting paper. He considered addressing it to an individual but concluded it would be futile. It had his signature at the bottom and that was all that was required.

Retrieving his pistol from the case he had placed under the bed required more effort, but the reduced gravity of the ship eased the task. He unlocked the door, then took the gun and his whiskey to the armchair and pulled himself across into its welcoming cushions. He checked the pistol carefully to ensure everything was in good working order, and loaded a single bullet. It wouldn't do to have a misfire, nor to have someone else accidentally fire it when they found him.

He took a long comforting mouthful of the whiskey and placed it on the side table. Raised the gun and placed it at his temple. And pulled the trigger.

CHAPTER 5

Travelling so fast through the sky from West to East had a curious effect on time. The seconds, minutes and hours became compressed. It felt like mid-afternoon as they cruised across the Indian Ocean and yet the sun already dipped toward the horizon.

Their table for the evening meal was barely half full as Maliha took her usual seat. She was not hungry since, in reality, lunch had not been very long ago. And it had been a very unpleasant lunch. Temperance was the only one who seemed in good humour as she helped herself to the food.

"So, the General did it," said Temperance. "Good riddance to the sodomite."

There was a sharp intake of breath from Valerie. Maliha was stunned by the remark, what was this? A factor in the murder of which she was not aware. Was the General a sodomite? With whom? Oh.

"Please, Miss Williams!" asked Max. "There is a lady present."

"I think you'll find," said Mr Crier. "There are three ladies present."

"I do not require you to defend me, Mr Crier," said Temperance. She pointed her knife at the Spencers. "You two are the worst type of snob. You're worse even than Mrs la-di-da Makepeace-Flynn. It's taken generations of breeding to make her into the cow she is today. You two have only your own bourgeois aspirations to blame."

Max stood up, grabbed his wife's hand and pulled her to her feet. "If you were a man, Miss Williams, I would demand satisfaction."

"If you were a man, Mr Spencer, I would oblige."

Max looked as though he might strain something looking for a suitable retort. He failed. "Come, Valerie," was all he could manage. He turned on his heel and stalked off with Valerie fluttering beside him.

"Thank the Lord," said Temperance, and returned to her meal.

"You are a curious missionary, Miss Williams," said Mr Crier. Her only response was to glance up at him, her eyes devoid of discernible emotion. He turned his attention to Maliha.

"So, Miss Anderson, what do you make of it all?"

"I do not believe I have anything to add, as I said at lunch." She attempted to make her statement as final as possible, but he seemed immune. She needed to think about this new idea, Lochana was a man?

"A queer business though. The General is having an affair with his nurse. That much is understandable given the disagreeable nature of his wife. But in a most sordid turn it seems his nurse was a man in disguise."

"It wasn't a disguise," Maliha said absently as memories surfaced of her old life at home; all the different people who visited and consulted her mother.

"I beg your pardon?"

"I was just saying it wasn't a disguise, Mr Crier." Maliha felt awkward as she had made herself the centre of attention, even Temperance was listening. "Sometimes, an Indian might feel they are in a body of the wrong sex. It's been a long time but I believe they are called Hijra."

"Ridiculous," said Temperance. "Primitive. Now you see why I am a missionary to these people, Mr Crier."

Mr Crier smiled and nodded in her direction. "Then something happens between them and he kills her."

"Yes, of course," said Maliha. "Except..." She trailed off, as thoughts played hide and seek in her mind. Silence hung about the table while, around them, the chink of crockery and scrapes of cutlery on porcelain went on.

"Except what?" demanded Temperance.

"I wonder what time she died?" Maliha said. "You saw her at six and no one saw her again. So the General probably didn't do it."

"That's what he wrote," said Mr Crier.

Maliha's eyes narrowed. "You've seen his suicide note?"

Maliha could almost read the excuses that ran through his mind as he thought of them and rejected them again. "I haven't seen it. I was told what it said."

She nodded. "I imagine he also said he had returned to his room after bridge and found her dead in his room. Realising the scandal that would ensue if he were to report it; he got the window open in his cabin and pushed the body of his lover out; expecting it to be gone forever."

"How did you know?"

"It only takes a logical mind, Mr Crier."

"I knew it was you," he said and Maliha's excitement drained away. "You were the one involved in the Taliesin Affair. They said it was a schoolgirl but never said who."

"I was not *involved*."

"You?" Temperance could not have been more incredulous. The revelation also caused her to frown, and she seemed to be contemplating something.

"If you'll excuse me," said Maliha. "I think I will retire." She rubbed her fingers absently on the napkin and dropped it beside her plate. She found Mr Crier ready to remove the chair from under her as she stood. There was nothing she could do to stop him, so she allowed it.

She did not look back as she headed for the salon door.

ii

Maliha pressed her back against her cabin door in a futile attempt to keep the world at bay. Would this nightmare trip never end? Now they knew she was the "schoolgirl investigator". She hated the journalists but for once her Anglo-Indian heritage had helped: they had not used her picture or her name.

But still. The General had stated he did not kill Lochana. It made sense because the timings were wrong; there was no motive and—she realised she had no idea how Lochana had been killed. Had she been shot with the General's gun? Or stabbed? Or even poisoned? Probably not poison, murder would be hard to prove. And a gunshot would doubtless have been heard unless it were done in the engine room, it was a sound that would reverberate and carry in the metal of the ship—just as it had with the General's suicide. Would a gunshot wound bleed more than a stabbing? Probably it would, if it were going to kill at all it would do a great deal of damage.

Most likely stabbed then. Sufficiently badly to be fatal but not enough to kill her immediately, she still had the strength to go from where she had been attacked to the General's cabin. It couldn't be too far or she would have been seen.

Maliha cried out and kicked the door with her heel. Not having full access to the facts that were clearly known to others was a significant disadvantage. She stopped at the thought. Turned and faced the mirror.

"What am I doing?" she asked her reflection, but her simulacrum looked as confused as she felt. "The General will be blamed for the murder, and they will wrap it up with a nice red bow. His wife will have to live with the social ignominy of being married to both a murderer and a sodomite. And the real murderer will go free."

She nodded at herself. It would be unfair if the General were to be found guilty of both crimes, though what befell Mrs Makepeace-Flynn was neither here nor there. But that the true murderer should go free? That could not be borne.

She would need to act quickly because as soon as the vessel was in radio range of Bombay they would report the murder, and police would come aboard as soon as they landed. If her previous experience was anything to go by they would settle for what was convenient and any further investigation would be stifled. Only a few hours remained.

With new purpose coursing through her, she equipped herself with a light jacket and a hat, pinning it firmly in place. She hefted her walking cane, she might not need it for walking, but it always lent her positive strength when dealing with others. Thus armoured she stepped through her cabin door and locked it.

iii

It was Mr Crier's custom to take a turn around the Observation Deck after meals. It took him a moment to recognise the lady striding purposefully in his direction swinging her cane. He almost started when he realised it was Miss Anderson. It looked like her, yet her demeanour was that of a different woman to the one he knew.

He touched his cap as she approached. "Good evening, Miss Anderson."

"Mr Crier. Please walk with me."

She walked past him without slowing. He had to overcome his momentum and almost run to catch her up.

"How can I assist you?"

"You must tell me everything you know about the death of Lochana Modi and General Makepeace-Flynn." He was quite taken aback at her demanding tone.

"Shall we have a drink?"

She stopped abruptly by ramming her cane into a ridge between the planks of the deck. Once more he was forced to dance to her tune as he sailed further along the deck and had to turn back. "This is not a social matter, Mr Crier. All I require is your information."

"Naturally I was not suggesting anything of that nature. I thought you might prefer somewhere a little more private."

Miss Anderson looked about at the scattered groups of individuals, families and couples promenading. "This is quite private enough," she paused, considering. "Perhaps if you were to offer me your arm we might continue. If you do not feel it would reflect badly upon you."

Mr Crier extended his arm and felt the lightest of touches as her thin fingers brushed his arm. She did not come in close, but that was to be expected. She was most certainly a strange woman.

"Where would you like me to start?"

"Do you know when Lochana is believed to have died?"

"I understand the best estimate is early evening but that the nature of her death makes it hard to judge accurately."

"And can I ask how you know this?"

"The doctor is an old school chum," he said. "May I ask why you want to know? This will not help the General now, or his wife. It can only cause more upset."

"The apprehension of the real murderer is paramount, wouldn't you say?"

He sighed. "What else do you want to know?"

"How was she killed? Was she stabbed? With what? And how many times?"

She sounded almost ghoulish in her demand for detail. "Yes, she was stabbed. It was something with a very thick blade and quite long."

"How many blows were delivered?"

"Only one, I believe."

She fell silent. He stopped and turned toward her pensive face. "I do apologise, are you feeling well?"

She returned from wherever she had been. "What? Unwell? No, of course not. The facts must be evaluated one against the other."

"It does not disgust you?"

"Of course, I am disgusted. Can you imagine the mind of someone who could commit such a crime?" She did not pause for an answer. "It is just a matter of considering the motive, means and opportunity. If they cannot be divined we only lack sufficient information."

She gestured to him to continue walking.

"Your involvement in the Taliesin Affair has given you a taste for mystery then?"

"I was not *involved*, Mr Crier. There was a great deal at stake and I was the only one to see it."

They had come around to the forward part of the deck and crossed in front of the Ladies Reading Room.

"Perhaps you would like to watch the sports?" he asked and paused for a reply that did not come.

Thin cloud hid the stars and all that could be seen of the moon was a whitish glow, but the electric lights kept the dark at bay across the deck. There were shouts and cheers from the game players. He walked on and she followed along with him.

Miss Anderson remained quiet, wrapped in a cocoon of thought. He had never before associated with a woman with such a power of concentration. It was almost unnerving. They approached the starboard stairwell. She finally spoke but "Ah" was all she said.

iv

Back in her room Maliha retrieved her reticule from where it lay in the dressing area. She poured a glass of water and switched on all the lights. With the glass beside her, she sat in the armchair with her reticule open in her lap. She pulled out the letter. The name on the outside *Lochan Modi* now made sense.

She broke the seal and withdrew a single sheet of folded paper. She examined the interior of the envelope briefly then discarded it. With delicate fingers she opened the letter and stared at the strange characters for a few moments then dropped it with a sigh. There were so many languages in India and as many different scripts to go with them. If she had been educated there she might have known this form of writing.

It was critical she speak with the steward who knew Lochana.

For the first time in the journey, she eyed the push button on the wall near the bed that would summon a member of the staff to her room but there was no guarantee he would be the one to respond.

She stuffed the letter back into her reticule and headed towards the stern lounge.

Beside the bar she paused and looked out across the empty room. All was quiet; far quieter than would be expected at this time of night. The deaths and the imminent arrival at Bombay had cleared the decks. Except for one chair, facing the huge windows, from which a thin line of cigarette smoke rose. On the small table next to it was a small glass of something green, a liqueur no doubt. The chair's occupant, however, was hidden by its high back.

"Can I help you?" The steward behind the bar was not the one she needed. He was English and sported the thin moustache favoured by the lower middle classes.

She turned to face him. "Yes. I need to speak to one particular steward. Indian by birth, I believe he came aboard at Khartoum, and his uniform is too large for him. Do you know him?"

The man's look was difficult to decipher but after a short pause he turned and went through a door into the back. Moments later he returned, followed by a nervous looking man, the very steward she required. Maliha glanced at the library door. The lamps inside were still lit.

"Come with me." She opened the door and entered. "Don't shut the door."

"Can I help, Sahiba?" He was sweating.

"What's your name?"

"Pravangkar Modi, Sahiba."

"You are family to Lochana?"

"Lochan was my brother, Sahiba."

Maliha removed the letter from her reticule and offered it. "Here."

He took it. "It is open."

"What does it say?"

"It tells that our father is dead. Lochan should help the family. He should send money."

"Nothing else?"

He shook his head. "Will you tell the Captain about me, Sahiba?"

"Were you on duty here yesterday evening?"

He nodded. "I deliver orders to rooms."

"Did you see anything?"

He shook his head and looked towards the door. "Why do you ask me these questions, Sahiba? Only bad things can happen."

"Do you want the murderer to go unpunished?"

He frowned. "The General?"

"Nonsense. Whatever you may think of his nature, or the nature of your brother, I saw them together. They loved each other. Besides the times are all wrong. So what did you see?"

He did not answer.

"If you do not tell me then I will tell the Captain of your connection to Lochana. What will they think then?"

Maliha was not proud of the shiver of terror that shook him as the thought sank in. After all, how much more convenient for the police to have an Indian as the murderer?

"Please do not, Sahiba. I beg you." He dropped his head and pressed his palms together fingers pointing toward her.

"Then tell me what you saw."

"I saw nothing of value, Sahiba. The engineer and his wife returning to their cabin."

"You mean the Spencers?"

He nodded.

"That is not unusual; they did not come to the lounge that evening. They said they were retiring." He shuffled his feet.

"What else?"

"Please, Sahiba…"

"Very well," she said, and took a step towards the door, he instantly looked relieved. "I will go straight to the Captain."

The relief turned to terror. "They went to their cabin!"

"But?"

"They went to another place first."

"Where?"

"I do not know—"

"Oh, for heaven's sake," she took another step towards the door. His arm snaked out, his hand gripping her forearm.

"They came from the passageway with your cabin, with the General's cabin, with Lochan's cabin. They were not coming from the salon."

She stopped, and his fingers fell from her arm. "What time was this?"

"Between nine and ten o'clock."

"How many minutes after nine?"

He thought for a moment. "Perhaps thirty or forty."

"Very good."

CHAPTER 6

Maliha hesitated at the door to Mrs Makepeace-Flynn's cabin. She was a
formidable and unpleasant woman at the best of times, and this was not the
best of times. However there was no alternative; the ship was only an hour
from Bombay. She knocked firmly then took a step back.

A few moments later the door was opened by a maid. Maliha recognised
her as one of the ship's crew. She was not Indian. "Can I help, Miss?" She
spoke with an over-emphasised "h" as if being particularly careful not to
drop it.

"Miss Anderson to see Mrs Makepeace-Flynn." She spoke loudly
enough that the General's wife would be able to hear her.

"Let her in," came the harsh voice from within. "And leave us. Come
back in the morning to pack." The maid stepped aside to allow Maliha in,
and then left shutting the door firmly.

The cabin barely differed from the others: same furnishings, same rug
and no windows as this was an interior room similar to the one
Temperance had. Barbara Makepeace-Flynn rose to her feet from the
armchair.

"What do you want?" she said. "Have you come to gloat?"

"It must be difficult."

"What?"

"Can I offer my sincere condolences, Mrs Makepeace-Flynn?"

She seemed taken aback, as if the fire in her had been extinguished. She
sat down.

Maliha noticed that tea had been brought but not served. She splashed a
small amount of milk from the delicate jug, poured the tea and passed it to
the older woman who took it almost without noticing. Maliha did not make
one for herself but perched on the edge of the sofa.

"It's a terrible thing to happen."

The General's widow ran her finger delicately around the rim of the tea
cup. Maliha could see her hand shaking.

"Forty-three years we were married," she said, almost talking to herself. "In all that time he never even held my hand. The last time he touched me was at the wedding ceremony when he put this ring on my finger." She held out her left hand and looked at it as if it did not belong to her. "Do you understand what I am saying?" She jerked her head up at Maliha who met her eye but only trusted herself enough to give a slight nod.

"I had no idea what he was really like. I was naive. We travelled so much: the soldier's life, y'know. I did what any good wife would do. I kept his house, and I waited for him."

She brushed her fingers against her cheek leaving a trail of dampness. "Then came the stories. You think I am harsh and cold, Miss Anderson, do you not? Don't deny it. That may be so but among officers' wives there is seldom great friendship. We do not remain in one place more than a year, and always there is the competition and the cutting tongue. So I came to hear the stories about my husband and his … preferences. And they laughed behind their false sympathy."

"But then, finally, after all those years of torture he succumbed to the wheelchair. Judge me how you may, Miss Anderson, but I was glad when he was shot because he would be mine at last." She went silent and took a sip from her cup.

Maliha wanted the whole story. "But that was not to be—"

"No! That was not to be, as you say." Her voice was acidic with anger and pain. "No, because he brought that woman … that nurse. Lochana Modi. And it was she that tended him. She who spent her hours looking after him. She who was with him day and night."

She looked up into Maliha's eyes again. "I hated her."

"But your husband loved her."

"Yes!" she hissed. "That much was obvious. I tried to console myself at first with the thought that, after all the stories and innuendo, at least he now loved someone of our sex." She gave a humourless laugh. "But that was false. She was a man after all. I did not kill that pervert, Miss Anderson, but I assure you I would have happily wrung her neck."

"I can't imagine how you felt."

"No. I doubt you can," she said. "When I was informed of her true nature, I felt as if I would break. And to have my husband enter at that very moment. To make a public scene."

"I am truly sorry."

The General's wife looked her in the eye. "I believe you are." She gave another half laugh, as lacking in humour as the other. "You are a surprising young woman, Miss Anderson. Most extraordinary." She paused and drained the tea cup in an undignified way then quickly dug out a kerchief to dab her eyes.

Maliha smiled gently. "Would you like more tea?"

ii

Through the port-side panorama of the Observation deck, Maliha watched the lights of Bombay glittering through the rain and the dark. It wasn't monsoon yet, if it had been she probably wouldn't have been able to see a thing.

Laid out before them was the rectangular landing dock, lit with the dazzling brilliance of dozens of electric lamps. Landing at night, and in the rain, would be nearly impossible without the lights. The rotors along the side of the ship had pivoted into their upright hover position and the ship drifted into place through its momentum and the guidance of smaller rotors located strategically around the ship's hull.

As they moved over the landing field she had to lean farther out to see below. The ship continued to descend. Whenever it drifted off station the sure hand of the Captain easily brought it back into position.

Below them she knew that hatches were being opened and sure enough the ground crew ran out through the torrent of rain and under the ship. She contemplated for a moment what would happen to a man if he were crushed by 35,000 tons of Sky Liner but then they reappeared running back from the ship holding the hawsers that had been thrown from the open hatches. These were rapidly attached to winches firmly anchored to the dock. The winches turned under steam power gathering up the slack in the lines.

Now began a battle the vessel did not intend to win. While the rotors were kept up to speed, the winches pulled the ship down towards the dock. The brilliant lights gleamed off the wings, turbine housings and rotors. Finally, when the Observation deck was no higher than the surrounding buildings, the power to the rotors was finally reduced and the ship settled the final few yards to the ground with barely a bump.

The ship's klaxon sounded three times in quick succession. Maliha grasped her walking stick firmly by its end and braced herself against it. On the bridge, the Captain gave the order and the Faraday device was deactivated. Maliha felt her full weight return and the pressure on her leg made it ache. The iron and steel of the ship groaned in sympathy as its weight settled.

Bombay. The seven islands of the archipelago had been subject to extensive land reclamation through the last two hundred years and were now almost all connected by broad land bridges. The port where the ship now rested, to the north east of the city, had been swamp only a few years before, and sea only a little before that.

She looked out into the city streets, lines of darkness delineated by dim gaslights. While in the distance, the frontages of the larger buildings were illuminated by electric lights. At first glance one might believe it was London or any other city in Britain with the grand Victorian buildings rising above the streets lined with lower three and four story structures. The railway station, not far away, was a slab of gothic architecture dwarfing the buildings around it.

But then you looked closer and saw the pillars and towers of the Jain temples that would never be seen in England, and the curiously garbed people passing occasionally under the street lights.

Under normal circumstances, those disembarking would leave the ship almost immediately; but not this time. Once the vessel was secured perhaps twenty Indian police officers emerged from a building marked Immigration. They deployed at a fast trot around the ship facing inward clearly to prevent anyone attempting to leave without permission.

After them came another group of men, one in the uniform of the P&O line, another in a brown suit and the remaining six being uniformed police. They crossed the distance to the ship and disappeared beneath it. Little doubt this was the Inspector and his men.

"An unpleasant night, Miss Anderson."

She turned. "Just a night like any other, Mr Crier."

He leaned on the rail and looked down at the loose circle of policemen, already dripping wet in the rain. "I fear those who are planning to leave are in for a long night, unless they managed to get to the front of the queue."

"Interviewing them is a waste of time and energy," she said following his gaze.

"Because you know who the murderer is?"

"Because they don't."

iii

It was six o'clock in the morning, Bombay time, when the *Macedonia* once more took to the air. Maliha remained asleep. She had not watched the slow trickle of passengers leaving the ship as each was interviewed briefly and allowed off. She was not aware of the fraying tempers and stern words.

An hour later she woke, dressed, breakfasted in the near-empty salon and—grateful for the reduced gravity once more—emerged for a short constitutional around the deck. She took her walking stick with her even though she did not need it.

The view from the Promenade deck revealed the Indian Ocean to the starboard dotted with fishing vessels and the occasional sea-bound steamer. To port and ahead, the ragged strip of the wide Indian coastal landscape was crisscrossed by rivers that mixed and separated in a great confusion while punctuated by villages and towns. Further inland was the mountain range that paralleled the coast and ran all the way to Kerala.

The Reading room was thankfully quite deserted. She was expecting a summons from the Inspector quite soon so there would be little point getting tied up in Shakespeare just now. However, as she had hoped, there were a dozen copies of *The Times of India* on a table.

She took a copy to a reading desk, her back to the window but facing the door.

She glanced at the front page. There was an article about the proposed Indian Press Act to limit what the native newspapers were permitted to cover. She was familiar with the story and *The Times* spoke in a similar way to the newspapers back in Britain: the natives were restless and could not be trusted, cut their ability to speak to the ignorant populace and their talk of revolution will be similarly suppressed.

She moved on. She read quickly, a talent that had earned her even more scorn at school from the teachers as well as her fellow pupils. She rapidly absorbed the local Bombay stories and those having wider importance. She reached page five and stopped.

TRAGIC ACCIDENT IN PUDUCHERRY

Her mother and father's names leapt from the page as the words of the article burned into her mind. *Fire … all dead.* A cold hand reached out and took hold of her heart. She could not move and stared at the words. The only image in her mind was her home with fire ripping through the wooden walls and floors.

"Miss Anderson?"

She jerked her head up. She had not noticed the three men enter. The moment of outrage at them entering the women's domain passed. This was not the *zenana* of an Indian household where a man could not enter.

"Yes." She blinked twice. She recognised the Inspector from last night. There were dark circles round his eyes, he was insufficiently shaven and his cheeks seemed to droop. "Inspector." She realised the man next to him was Mr Crier, which was somewhat surprising; then again perhaps it was not. The man behind was one of the policemen, a sergeant by his stripes, and he looked equally tired.

She looked down at the newspaper article again, hoping vainly it had been nothing but a fancy. The words still sat on the page. She inhaled deeply, held it for a moment and breathed out.

She took hold of herself, forced herself to stand and held out her hand to shake. An action which took the Inspector aback but he rallied and took hers in a loose grip. She could feel calluses on his hand; he had seen hard manual labour in his time.

"Inspector Forsyth, Miss. I'd like to ask you a few questions."

His Glaswegian accent was a further shock. He sounded just like her father.

"Yes, of course."

He led the way to a group of leather settees. They arranged themselves at an appropriate distance from one another. The sergeant remained standing.

Forsyth's questions were the standard sort one came to expect from the police: times, places, what was seen, questions about relationships. Normal, of course, if one had come into contact with the police before, which she had. Then came the one she was expecting.

"Mr Crier here tells me you're the young lady behind the Jordan case."

She found herself warming to the Inspector. He did not use the sensationalist title the press had attached to the event in Brighton.

"Yes."

"You're a little young, aren't you?"

"I am nineteen, Inspector. I did not have a particularly demanding social life at my school, as you may imagine. Thus I had much free time and I read a great deal. I believe this gave me a suitable grounding."

"And you have been investigating this case?"

No point in denying it with Mr Crier sitting there. "Yes."

"And what conclusion have you reached?"

"That General Makepeace-Flynn did not kill Lochana Modi, and if we reach the Fortress without apprehending the real murderer they will escape scot-free."

"Can you prove he did not do it?"

"There was no motive; no sign of a murder weapon, let alone any idea what it might have been; and the opportunity aspect is uncertain."

"But you cannot prove he did not do it."

"No one can prove a negative, Inspector."

"So do you know who did it?"

"I think so. But I cannot prove that either yet."

"So who do you think it is?"

"I'm sorry, Inspector. I can't tell you."

He frowned. "And why not, Miss Anderson?"

"You won't believe me," she replied. "However you may find it useful to ask the Spencers what they were doing lurking around our cabins the night Lochana was killed."

"You think they did it?"

"I doubt it. But you can be sure they have something interesting to tell you."

iv

The Inspector had left her and gone about his business—probably to make life difficult for the Spencers—leaving her in the Reading room. Now she simply stood and stared out at the landscape drifting by. But she saw none of it, the death of her parents had numbed her. Her fingers curled around the railing were cold.

All these months, years even, she had dreamed of going home, it was the one thing that made school tolerable and now there was no home to return to. Her father's estate would go to someone in Glasgow who would not even want to know her. And if he had been conscientious enough to make his will then anything left to her would be in trust for the next two years, if she ever managed to see a penny of it.

"It's an amazing land."

Maliha did not turn at Temperance's voice. All she wanted was to shut herself away, from everyone and everything but she did not have energy to move.

"Miss Anderson, you are crying."

Am I? she thought. She raised a hand to her cheek and touched the wetness. *So I am.*

"Whatever is the matter, *cariad*?"

Maliha choked as she tried to suppress a sob.

"Was it that policeman? Men have no feelings."

Maliha shook her head. "No… no, not him."

"Come on, let's get you somewhere private," said Temperance and put her arm around Maliha's shoulders. "You can't go making a spectacle of yourself. Not when you're almost home."

Her solicitations forced another bout of sobs from Maliha. Temperance turned her toward the door. The room was now quite busy and the spinsters and debutantes were looking.

"My walking stick," said Maliha pointing back towards the rail. Temperance walked back and picked it up, putting it gently into Maliha's hands before guiding her through the door, across the deck and below to her cabin.

CHAPTER 7

Temperance unlocked the door and pushed it open. "In you go now, *cariad.*"

She studied Maliha as she stepped into the dark interior just inches from her, breathing in the soap-smell of her skin. She followed Maliha inside, switched on the light, shut the door and turned the key gently so as not to alarm her guest. The room was a mess. She had left her empty cases open on the bed ready for packing and her sewing box was still open on the desk.

They would be landing in only a few hours but there was still time.

Maliha had stopped a few paces into the room, so she gently took her by the elbow and guided her to the sofa and settled her into it. She relieved her of her walking stick and placed it along the side of the sofa just out of Maliha's reach.

"Shall I send for tea?" she asked.

"Just some water, if you don't mind."

"We don't want to be disturbed, now do we?"

Temperance went to the glass-fronted drinks cabinet. She had resisted the temptation to pour every last drop of the foul liquor into the basin lest the servants think she had drunk it herself. She folded down the front, took out a lead crystal tumbler and poured water from the jug. She hated the way it moved so sluggishly, it was so unnatural.

She looked at the reflection in the glass as she put down the jug. She saw her dress-making scissors in Maliha's hands with the blades wide apart. She seemed to be examining them. Temperance smiled, it would be amusing to catch her in the act.

"Do you sew?" she said.

Maliha shook her head and put the scissors back. Temperance sat down beside her, passed her the glass and placed her hand on Maliha's. She had beautifully delicate fingers, but her skin was cold.

"Why don't you tell me what is wrong, *cariad?*"

Temperance saw the tears well up again. Poor thing was in such terrible need.

"Have you a kerchief?" Maliha asked sniffing indecorously.

Temperance stood up and went to the dresser; she took a handkerchief from one of the smaller drawers and switched on the bedside light. Then went to the door and switched off the main lights. She did not mind that her cabin did not have more windows as darkness brought her closer to God. As she turned back, she noticed Maliha staring at the small window as if she had seen something. Temperance pulled the small curtain across it.

"Here you are." She passed Maliha the kerchief and watched as she delicately wiped the tears from her cheeks. She sat down close beside her, feeling the comfort of Maliha's thigh pressing against hers. But she was not the one in need of solace. She placed her arm around Maliha's shoulders and rested the other on her leg. She knew from many years of experience that those in grief were the easiest to manipulate. Listen to their sorrows, give them succour and they could be commanded.

In her quietest but most insistent voice she asked again. "Tell me what has happened."

Temperance allowed the silence to stretch out. Sometimes it took a while for them to gather the courage to speak.

"It was in the paper. My parents are dead. My home is burned," said Maliha. "I have no parents and no home."

Temperance almost laughed, it was such a common story, but now was not the time for laughing. That would come later. "And no income I'll wager."

Maliha shook her head. "I don't know what the arrangements are. It was only a newspaper."

The two of them remained silent for a time. Temperance watched her, seeing the downcast eyes, still on the verge of tears, felt her confidence grow. The girl had not thrown off her arm she even seemed to be nestling deeper into the embrace, nor had she removed the hand from her leg which should be considered a great impertinence.

Temperance kissed Maliha's cheek. Maliha closed her eyes. Temperance's heart leapt with joy. She had not been rejected. So many times she had been and the pain was hard to bear.

She opened her eyes and turned to face Temperance. Maliha's eyes, still glistening with tears, looked searchingly into her own. Their lips almost touching, preparing for that first kiss.

Maliha spoke: "It must have been a terrible shock when you discovered Lochana was a man."

ii

Temperance's arm about her shoulders became rigid, and the hand on her thigh tightened. Maliha pulled away from Temperance so she could see her full face more clearly in the half light. The look of excitement had been replaced by confusion, and something much harder and sharper.

"What?" Temperance's voice grated as if someone had gripped her throat.

"You killed her because you found out she was a man."

Temperance jerked away from Maliha as if she were poison. She jumped to her feet, grabbed her cigarette holder from the table and put it in her mouth even though it contained no cigarette. Then removed it again in annoyance.

"The General killed the pervert," she said. "Everyone knows that. You are weak in the head."

"No, he did not. He loved her."

"Love?" she screamed. "Thou shalt not lie with a man as with a woman; that is an abomination."

"The fact remains. He cared for her. He did not kill her. He could not have. You did."

Temperance fumbled with her cigarette case, jammed a cigarette into the holder and lit it. She took in a deep breath of smoke, blew it out and felt its energy flowing through her, calming her. She laughed and sat down facing Maliha.

"You're a very dull girl, you know? You think you're so clever with all your books. Well if you remember I was reading your Shakespeare in the lounge all afternoon until dinner."

Temperance sat as if tied. Ankles and knees tight together, elbows pulled in.

"That was to cover the tryst you had arranged with her. Lochana was found dead in the same clothes as she'd worn into Khartoum. If she had been killed in the evening she would have changed. No. You arranged to meet with her immediately after your excursion. The chairs in the lounge are big enough that you could leave your cigarette holder there, with a drink and anyone would think someone was sitting there."

Temperance glanced at her cigarette holder. Then back at Maliha. "Or I was sitting there reading all afternoon. And you're wrong. I saw her in the evening she said she was going for a walk."

"You made that up to confuse matters," said Maliha.

"You dare to accuse me of lying," she cried. "I do God's work."

But Maliha would not be side-tracked. "You came back to this room where she was waiting. And you … discovered she was a man and in a rage you grabbed up the nearest thing you could and you stabbed her. You thought you'd killed her then and there, and went to cover your tracks. But when you came back she was gone."

"You can't prove any of this. You're an ignorant half-caste daughter of a demented father."

Maliha ignored the insult. It hurt to be reminded of her father but the girls at school had been far more imaginative with years of experience.

She changed tack. "Where's your rug?"

"What?" Temperance looked down at the bare deck and then at the door. "There wasn't one."

"All the cabins have rugs, Temperance," said Maliha. "You got rid of it because it was stained with Lochana's blood. The seals are broken on one of the outer windows in the companionway outside; you threw it out the same way the General disposed of her body. I noticed when the Master-At-Arms was examining the General's room."

Temperance sat back, her muscles loosening. She took another deep drag on the cigarette holder, held the smoke in her lungs then blew it out smoothly. "You still have no proof, Miss Anderson."

"That's true, everything up to now is strongly indicative that you killed her but not an absolute certainty. Except you made a mistake. An independently verifiable mistake."

"I don't make mistakes," she said.

"You made a mistake with me, didn't you? You thought I would succumb to your seduction, but I have to say, you are not my type."

Temperance leapt to her feet and slapped Maliha across the face so fast, she had no time to pull back. "Not your type? You ugly little whore. I do God's work. I give God's love where it will best serve His purpose."

Maliha's cheek stung, and she almost regretted the moment of facetiousness. But again, she hadn't survived school without more than her share of physical mistreatment. A slap was nothing.

"So what was my big mistake?" demanded Temperance.

iii

The pathetic little girl held her hand against her cheek. She had to die, of course: she would not accept the absolution of God's love. She could not be allowed to prevent the spreading of the Truth. Maliha was nothing but a disgusting half-breed.

Temperance took a long pull on her cigarette. It relaxed her. She saw her scarf on a hook on the far wall. Stabbing may not kill someone fast enough but choking the living breath from her would be effective and satisfying.

She strode across the room and took the silk scarf delicately in her hands. She loved its sensuous feel.

"Well? What was my mistake?"

It was almost as if Maliha accepted her fate. She did not turn about as Temperance twisted the scarf into a tight band.

"You told Mrs Makepeace-Flynn about Lochana."

She could not have erred. "It was common knowledge."

"When you told her no one outside of the crew knew."

"She told me herself." Yes, that was it, the pervert had revealed the truth to her.

"No, she didn't. For two reasons: In the first instance she did not consider herself to be male; and second, you hate men. If you had known, you would not have given her time of day."

No. She could not have made a mistake. The little half-breed needed to die.

iv

In the dim light, a scarf whipped over her head and tightened about Maliha's neck. The pain shot through her along with the terrifying knowledge she could no longer breathe.

Temperance hissed in her ear. "Little Miss Goody Two-Shoes. Let me help you to Hell where you'll find your dead mother and father." Maliha tried to pull the cord from her neck but it was too tight, too thin, she could

- 63 -

not grip it. Spots danced before her eyes and there was a rushing in her ears. The muscles in her chest desperately tried to drag air into her lungs but could only spasm uselessly.

It would be so easy to just let go, why bother fighting? What was there about her life that really mattered? Then she remembered the child jumping high to touch the ceiling. And, as the noose tightened still more, Maliha reached back with both hands and gripped Temperance's dress. She hooked her heels under the sofa and hauled as hard as she could. With her grip so tight on the scarf Temperance lifted from the deck and turned vertically in the air.

The pressure lessened on Maliha's throat as Temperance descended in front of her, facing away. She crashed to the floor and released her grip on the scarf. Maliha took in a grating, howling breath as Temperance tried to regain her feet. Maliha grabbed her walking stick, brought it up and then down in a sideways sweep that cracked against Temperance's temple.

The murderess collapsed to the floor. Maliha drew a second breath that rasped through her crushed windpipe. Temperance moved her arms, trying to gain purchase and climb to her feet. Maliha swiped her head with her stick again as hard as she was able. And again. Temperance went limp. Maliha felt great satisfaction in the act though she was sure she would regret her gratuitous behaviour later.

Then the door broke open and two police constables fell into the cabin. The Inspector and Mr Crier stood in the doorway, and behind them Lochana's brother.

v

Maliha stood in the corner of her cabin watching two maids packing her things. She had not wanted any fuss, but the Captain had been insistent. He assured her that both he and the P&O line would be forever in her debt. It was a kind thought, but she doubted it. The company's executives would want to forget the whole affair as quickly as possible. Still, she was not ungrateful for the help. Her neck was very bruised, and she wore a high-necked blouse to hide the marks.

The only good thing to come out of this would be that she would be able to disembark well before the press got hold of the story. She was content to let the Inspector take the credit. The dried blood in the hinge of the scissors had settled the matter once and for all. The last thing Maliha wanted was her name involved, and the connection made to the Jordan case. She would never hear the end of it.

Someone appeared at the open door, hesitated then knocked.

"Yes, Mr Crier?"

He put his head around the door. "Good afternoon."

"Can I help you?"

"It has been suggested on more than one occasion that I am quite beyond help, Miss Anderson."

"What do you want?"

He glanced at the maids. "Shall we take a turn about the deck? For old time's sake?"

vi

"You do not have your stick," he said as they reached the Observation deck. The sun beat down through the glass ceiling.

"I don't require it when we are underway."

"And yet you had it with you when you confronted the monster."

Maliha did not reply. She touched her fingers to her neck.

"You are an extraordinary young woman, Miss Anderson."

She felt that comment too was best left unremarked.

They reached the port rail and looked out. The vessel was equidistant between India behind and Ceylon ahead. Halfway to the horizon two spits of land—one from each coast— reached out to one another but did not quite reach. But British industry was dealing with that issue: the pontoons of a nascent bridge were taking shape.

"Will you be returning to Puducherry?"

"There will be legal matters to deal with."

"Will you stay there?"

"I cannot say." There was nothing left there except memories and she carried the best of those with her.

"Do you have money?"

"I'm not sure that question is entirely appropriate, Mr Crier."

"But if you are in need…?"

She turned to face him, her face quite stern. "I am quite capable of looking after myself."

"Of that, I have no doubt."

She turned away again. "Besides, Barbara has offered me a room until such time as my future is known."

"Barbara? You mean Mrs Makepeace-Flynn?"

"The very one."

"You are indeed remarkable," he said. "To have tamed that beast. So you will be staying near the Fortress?"

"That remains to be seen," she said. *Once I have decided what on earth I am to do.*

i

One disadvantage of disembarking was that you did not get to see the place from the air as the ship approached. Instead Maliha was in the depths of the ship in the wide disembarkation lounge with the other first class passengers.

Her baggage had been collected and, together with Mrs Makepeace-Flynn—dressed in a mourning black veil—she had descended three flights into the main cargo area which contained, via a carpeted and enclosed companionway, the disembarkation lounge. Despite the very best efforts to make the lounge comfortable, the throbbing of the nearby engines and the heat of the furnaces could not be kept entirely at bay.

The lounge did not lack in facilities. There was the bar, leather chairs and sofas, and staff constantly checking to ensure all their needs were satisfied. But still she was reminded of her trip to Brighton one Saturday morning and how she had stumbled on the cattle market. She had seen the animals penned tight ready for sale and slaughter. It was not their ultimate destination that concerned her, it was the conditions they had to endure to get there.

Of those people she had met during the journey, only Mrs Makepeace-Flynn remained. It had come out the Spencers had seen Lochana staggering from Temperance's cabin to the General's but they had kept quiet. What they were doing in corridors away from their own while everyone else was at dinner she did not know and was apparently something the police were investigating, as a result they were not disembarking with the rest.

Temperance was in the ship's brig awaiting transport back to Bombay with Detective Forsyth. Now that all had been revealed she was quite unrepentant. There was little doubt she and the gallows would become intimately acquainted very soon. It was difficult to understand how a person could be so broken.

The one person unexpectedly missing was Mr Crier. She had not seen him since he had taken his leave of her this morning. She imagined he perceived their relationship as some sort of ship-board romance. She could not deny being flattered, such a thing had never occurred to her before, but the idea was ridiculous.

ii

Her introspection was interrupted as the ship's klaxon sounded three times in quick succession, and those standing in the lounge made for their seats. A few young men remained standing in an attitude of bravado while children were called and grabbed. Mrs Makepeace-Flynn adjusted her posture in anticipation. Maliha ensured her walking stick was to hand.

The Faraday device was disengaged and she sank deeper into her chair. There were various exclamations from around the lounge as full weight returned. She glanced about to see one of the young men climbing to his feet, a look of chagrin on his face. More disconcerting was the groaning of the ship's structure as it settled. At this position in the depths of the vessel was quite alarming.

Those disembarking on foot formed orderly lines but Maliha waited with Mrs Makepeace-Flynn until a steward arrived to tell them their carriage had arrived. They followed the steward to an area filled with horse-drawn carriages driven aboard to collect the passengers. Her earlier assessment of the state of the Makepeace-Flynn's finances was further evidenced by the old-style growler waiting for them, now loaded with their baggage. It was drawn by a pair of chestnuts.

On the far side of the area, a hearse waited to collect the General's body. It was not in burial colours, that would come later, but the four black horses stood waiting. One of them pawed the ground in boredom.

As the carriage descended the ramp, the hot dry air invaded the inside. The afternoon sun beat down and the temperature in the carriage became intense as they drove out across the vast commercial landing field. There were another two large passenger ships on the ground some distance away along with some smaller cargo ships of different design. They exited the field between large administrative buildings and the Fortress came into view.

iii

It was named *Sigirya* in Sinhalese, the native tongue of Ceylon, which meant "Fortress in the Sky". It had been acquired by the Empire to become the

Royal Navy's prime base because of its position roughly equidistant from Britain's main concerns: Britain, South Africa, and Australia while mainland India provided the workforce that Ceylon itself could not. And because of its position relative to the equator it was a similar distance to the Queen Victoria void station above.

Sigirya was a lump of rock—it could not be described otherwise—jutting six hundred feet from the flat landscape around it. It was encased with modern buildings that towered the same distance again. Encircling it at various heights were artillery guns on platforms.

Surrounding the Fortress itself was the Compound: a roughly circular area with a diameter of over two miles. Apart from the commercial port, there was the Naval Shipyard; a hospital that catered for both military and civilian needs; and the British Army had one segment containing barracks and training ground. The Governor's residence had been relocated from Columbo ten years earlier and was now surrounded by a residential area for the great and good. Barbara's home was one of them.

The whole compound was contained within a concrete wall. The whole structure was reminiscent of a medieval castle but on a massive scale.

And outside the Compound all manner of shops and houses created by those who could not live in the Compound but serviced its other needs.

A shadow passed over the carriage. She looked up. A vessel bearing the black cross of the Imperial German Sky Service blocked the sun. The Zeppelins utilised the Faraday Effect but used gas for their lift and only used engines for driving and manoeuvring. It was more efficient but had its risks. It was probably heading for, or returning from, German New Guinea with a refuelling stopover at the Fortress.

Mrs Makepeace-Flynn also looked out and up. Then sat back.

"Can you see if that's the *Hansa*, my dear?"

Maliha squinted up. The gothic German lettering was difficult to make out against the bright sky.

"Yes, I think so."

"Ah, good. We shall have some company tonight. Captain Voss is a cousin."

Maliha sat back in the carriage. Barbara's kind offer of accommodation was very welcome but this place stood on the edge of a war that was certain to come. There was nowhere for her to go, but how could she remain here?

Read this next

Maliha Anderson returns in *Blood Sky at Night.*

Find it at **http://bit.ly/maliha-02**

Steve Turnbull has been a geek and a nerd longer than those words have had their modern meaning.

Born in the heart of London to book-loving working class parents in 1958, he lived with his parents and two much older sisters lived in two rooms with gas lighting and no hot water. In his fifth year, a change in his father's fortunes took them out to a detached house in the suburbs. That was the year Dr Who first aired on British TV and Steve watched it avidly from behind the sofa. It was the beginning of his love of science fiction.

Academically Steve always went for the science side but he also had his imagination and that took him everywhere. He read through his local library's entire science fiction and fantasy selection, plus his father's 1950s *Astounding Science Fiction* magazines. As he got older he also ate his way through TV SF like *Star Trek*, *Dr Who* and *Blake's 7*.

However it was when he was 15 he discovered something new. Bored with a Maths lesson he noticed a book from the school library: *Cider with Rosie* by Laurie Lee. From the first page he was captivated by the beauty of the language. As a result he wrote a story longhand and then spent evenings at home on his father's electric typewriter pounding out a second draft, expanding it. Then he wrote a second book. After that he switched to poetry and turned out dozens, mostly not involving teenage angst.

After receiving excellent science and maths results he went on to study Computer Science. There he teamed up with another student and they wrote songs for their band - Steve writing the lyrics. Though they admit their best song was the other way around, with Steve writing the music.

After graduation Steve moved into contract programming but was snapped up a couple of years later by a computer magazine looking for someone with technical knowledge. It was in the magazine industry that Steve learned how to write to length, to deadline and to style. Within a couple of years he was editor and stayed there for many years.

During that time he married Pam (who also became a magazine editor) who he'd met at a student party.

Though he continued to write poetry all prose work stopped. He created his own magazine publishing company which at one point produced the subscription magazine for the *Robot Wars* TV show. The company evolved into a design agency but after six years of working very hard and not seeing his family—now including a daughter and son—he gave it all up.

He spent a year working on miscellaneous projects including writing 300 pages for a website until he started back where he had begun, contract programming.

With security and success on the job front, the writing began again. This time it was scriptwriting: features scripts, TV scripts and radio scripts. During this time he met a director Chris Payne, who wanted to create steampunk stories and between them they created the Voidships universe, a place very similar to ours but with specific scientific changes.

With a whole universe to play with Steve wrote a web series, a feature film and then books all in the same Steampunk world and, behind the scenes, all connected.

Join my mailing list at **http://bit.ly/voidships**

Made in the USA
Charleston, SC
15 October 2015